THE DEVIL'S OWN is an unstoppable story that hooks you right from the start. This spellbinding debut will make K.A. Fox one of your new favorite authors. A must read for all lovers of dark fantasy.

—Jessica Therrien,
best-selling author of
Children of the Gods

For Tony and the 3Gs – we did it.

THE DEVIL'S OWN

K.A. FOX

The Devil's Own

First Edition
Copyright © 2019 K.A. Fox

Book interior formatted and copy editing by Debra Cranfield Kennedy

www.acornpublishingllc.com

ISBN—Hardcover 978-1-947392-49-6
ISBN—Paperback 978-1-947392-48-9

CHAPTER ONE

THE RED SEQUINS at the top of my corset dug into my pale skin. I silently cursed the sizing guide that had suggested this might actually fit. The horned headband holding back the blonde curls I wore was giving me a headache, and I seriously considered smacking the next guy who grabbed at my tail. But, this was the job and I had to stick it out.

I'd been working the floor at the Gentlemen's Club in Angel Falls, Minnesota for weeks and I was still coming up empty. The man I was looking for was a no-show—again.

As the music came to an end, the DJ's voice came over the speakers. "Our next dancer, Marie, has a special request for her first song tonight. Let's everyone raise our glasses in honor of *Angus Murphy and The Law*—this is their song, 'The Devil's Own'."

It had been ten years since the band's plane had crashed and people still acted like they had just died yesterday. I couldn't deny their music had been good, but this sort of memorial was an annual ritual *everywhere* on Halloween. As a guitar riff replaced the DJ, everyone in the club stood, lifting their drinks in a solemn toast. I worked my way through the heavy crowd, skirting between people. The floor was slick with spilt alcohol and I was careful to avoid even the most casual touch.

At the bar, I entered drink orders, then slid away into the corner while they were prepared. The exposed brick of the walls dug into my bare shoulders, but this vantage point gave me the best view of the entire room. Men clustered up around the stage, their eyes laser-focused on Marie. We might have only met weeks ago, but in that time, she'd talked nonstop about her dreams of using the money she earned dancing to open her own yoga studio someday and regularly practiced poses in between her sets on the stage. Much to the men's, and her bank account's delight, she wasn't afraid to use some of those moves to her advantage on the pole.

The music built up to a crescendo at the chorus. Despite my ambivalent feelings, I couldn't keep myself from singing along quietly.

> *You can make the deal, roll the dice,*
> *but I'll give you one piece of advice.*
> *There's nowhere to run, no place you can go,*
> *you'll always be the Devil's own.*

A flare of heat ran along my skin. It was the first hint I'd had that my prey might finally be showing himself. I let my eyes wander through the crowd, wishing I knew what this man looked like. His face was always blurred in the security footage from the previous murders; a hint this murderer wasn't strictly human. Magic had let him hide his face as he hunted women down. Even so, I'd traced the pattern of death to Angel Falls. The heat on my skin built steadily, an itch working its way across my stomach. He was getting closer.

My eyes landed on a man, alone, skirting the edges of the crowd where pool tables were scattered. It looked like he'd just walked in the door, droplets of misty rain still shining in his short hair. His leather jacket and clothing were dark, letting him blend in with the shadows as he moved. His eyes were targeted on Marie, watching every move she made on the stage, never even drifting to anyone else. I kept my attention on him, watching as he passed under a small light that lit him up for a brief second. Red highlights flashed within his dark brown hair. This had to be the man I'd been searching for.

He stopped near a door to the private dance room, but didn't go in. He stood there like a statue, with an eerie stillness that made me think of violence coiled inside him, waiting to strike. I marked his location and turned back to the bartender who was waving me over. My orders were up. I straightened my horns and the nametag I wore that read JANEY, close enough to my own name that I wouldn't fail to respond when someone hollered it at me. One last deep breath. The time had come to head back out and play my part.

I worked my way around, delivering drinks even as I kept my attention on the man I'd been waiting for. He was still in place, watching the stage, his eyes never leaving Marie. As much as I itched to end the hunt while he was distracted, I was acutely aware of the security cameras above, always watching. No one could suspect I was anything other than what I'd claimed to be.

As Marie's final song came to an end, the closing notes were drowned out by the loud voices of two large men near the stage. The shouting escalated into pushing and shoving. Their friends jumped in, the tension in the air instantly ratcheting up. Security came running and pushed me off to the side as punches started flying. I pretended to lose my balance, wobbling on my high heels. Someone yanked on my tail and I fell backwards, the remaining drinks on my tray launching up into the air before crashing down on top of me as I landed in a man's lap, his hands groping at me, his skin touching mine.

That momentary contact was enough. Hunger surged up in me, and the ever-present shield I kept in place wavered. The temptation to feed myself from this man's energy swamped me. That starving piece inside me expanded, pleading for even a small taste. I could smell the soap he'd used earlier in the day comingled with sweat from a hard day of physical work and tobacco smoke. The instinct that made me this way promised it would be delicious if I would only give in. I almost did. But the fury swirling in my chest was stronger. I fought through the haze of need, focused on the reason I was there.

I tried to regain my feet, but the man grabbed at me, holding me in place. I threw my head back, appreciating the sound of his nose cracking on contact. He wailed, his hands releasing me as he cradled his face, and I jumped away from him. The place had become a free-for-all. Bartenders rushed onto the floor to break up fights. I forced my way around throngs of people, using my tray as a shield when necessary. The stage was the only clear spot, so I climbed up, using one of the poles as leverage and then sliding across to the other side. The club raged around me.

Just like before, I thought. *Utter chaos.* That's when I knew. The murderer I'd been hunting all this time had to be a Chaos Demon.

Panic coursed through me when I found the dressing room empty. I raced to the back door the dancers used when they wanted to go outside to smoke, shoving against the push bar. The door flew wide and I stepped out, letting it slam shut behind me. The sound echoed off the brick walls of the dimly lit alleyway. I knew from scouting the place there were no cameras for me to worry about. A low moan off to the side captured my attention. In the shadows of the far corner, the man I'd spent months trying to track down spun to face me, a small figure behind him shrinking against the wall.

"Hey!" I yelled to distract him from his prey. "Get away from her!"

Chaos stepped toward me. Eyes that had seemed so normal inside flashed an unearthly red light for a brief moment. I backed away a couple steps, baiting him into following me. With a little distance, I could kill him without worrying about Marie being hurt . . . or seeing something she shouldn't.

I kept moving, maintaining the space between us until he stepped into the light from the flickering halogen overhead, illuminating his facial features; strong nose, chiseled cheekbones, sharp jaw. His lips were pulled back, fangs bared. Growling low in his throat, he rushed at me, hands grasping my upper arms. He had almost a foot of height on me and significant pounds. I let his weight carry me down, rolling with the momentum, pushing him off me and launching him into the air. He crashed against the dumpster. As he gained his footing, I stood, balancing myself to prep for his next assault.

"You little bitch. I'm gonna enjoy cutting you into little pieces!" He growled and charged at me again. He was fast, but I was ready and slid to the right, grabbing his arm and swinging him up against the wall, grinning as I heard his chin smacking against the bricks. I bent his arm until his shoulder popped, noting the pained sound that escaped him. I kicked the back of his knee, causing it to collapse, dropping him down to the floor of the alleyway.

"Who are you?" he asked.

"Just someone who doesn't like what you do to women," I said. "And now you'll know exactly how it feels to be on the receiving end."

I had my knee on his back, weight centered to maintain my advantage. But I wasn't ready when he tensed under me, then reared back. I lost my grip on his arm and fell off to the left, landing on something soft and wet. Chaos swung around and grabbed my foot, dragging me toward him. My back scraped against the pavement, leaving behind a trail of bloody sequins and skin. His claws sank into my bare leg, the liquid trickle of blood starting to run. I caught my breath to fight the scream that threatened to escape. I grasped at the ground, but there was nothing to stop my slide. Then he was straddling me, strong thighs holding me in place while his hands worked their way to my throat. His eyes glittered, pinpricks of red coming and going as he began to squeeze, tighter and tighter. I bucked, trying to suck in air. He laughed at my efforts.

"That's right. Fight me, little girl. I enjoy it when you fight." His voice was like acid burning in my ears. I balled my left hand into a fist and swung it at his head. The connection with his cheekbone sent a shock up my arm, but the impact broke his concentration enough that I was able to suck in a few quick breaths. Shaking his head to clear it, Chaos stayed on top of me, his body weight holding me down even as I thrashed. He sneered, grabbing my left wrist and pinning it down, grinding it into the pavement. The long fingers of his free hand wrapped effortlessly around my small neck and pressed down again. Black specks began to cluster at the edge of my vision. I jerked and tried to scream but there was no air. He leaned in a little closer, laughing. "Just a little longer. Then I'll enjoy eating you bit by bit. While you're still alive. Two for the price of one."

Drops of his saliva landed on my face as I shoved against him once more. His eyes were locked with mine. I bucked up, less strength in me this time. He easily shrugged off my weak attempts to shake him loose. The sounds of my feet scratching along the rough ground as I tried to find some traction were loud in my ears, desperate as I fought to reach the handle of the blessed blade hidden in my boot. Chaos never looked away from my face, his attention focused intently on me. My vision darkened, blackness edging around the image of him above me. A sick smile crawled across his face, bone white teeth bared. "Soon," he leaned down to whisper at me, "I'll have you both." His tongue snaked out, licking my cheek and laughing in my ear.

The pop of air when I jammed my knife into his neck was sublimely satisfying. His mouth opened to gasp, choking on blood as the color drained from his face. Words I didn't understand gurgled out of him, but the rush of blood drowned his voice as he slid off to my side. I crawled out from under his legs, kicking them off and rolling onto my knees. I forced myself to take deep breaths, fighting the urge to hyperventilate. I heard a scrambling sound behind me and twisted around, my hands up in guard. It was just Marie, struggling to get to her feet.

I crawled over to her, not yet ready to try walking. She was hurt but alive. "Oh my God," she said, her voice weak. "He was going to kill me."

I nodded as she pointed at the collapsed shape on the ground behind me, her hands shaking. "Don't look," I said, my throat aching even with those simple words. "Don't look."

She sagged against the wall. Her knees were drawn up tight and she rested her arms against them as she covered her face with her hands. I turned back to where our attacker lay, motionless in a dark spreading pool. His dead eyes appeared human once again. The red sparks that had lit his eyes were gone, his fangs retracted. When the police found us in the alley, they led Marie away to be treated for her injuries. I closed my eyes as her cries rose to a panicked height. At least this part was over.

CHAPTER TWO

SITTING IN THE interview room of the Angel Falls Police Department, I tried to stay warm. Someone had lent me a jacket, but I was still shivering. I wrapped my arms around my middle, hoping to hold in whatever body heat I might have and stave off the shakes threatening to take over. I was tired and dirty, parts of me still spattered with blood. I was ready for a hot shower and pain medicine. My eyes closed, I slowed my breathing until I felt in control again.

When the door finally opened, I was surprised the man who walked in set a chipped mug of steaming liquid in front of me before he dropped down in the chair across the table. I wrapped my stiff fingers around the warm ceramic, sniffing cautiously.

"Tea?" I asked.

"Your friends mentioned you're not much of a coffee drinker. They seem to think it's pretty cute you're hooked on this stuff instead."

I nodded, then sipped carefully. It was heaven. "Thank you."

"Least I could do after what you went through," he said. "I'm Detective Bishop."

"I'm Janey, but you already know that."

"True. Talked with your boss about you and the other girl, Marie." His gaze flicked over me and I held still even though I hated the scrutiny. "You're twenty-four, started at the club about a month or so ago. Everyone says you're quiet, stay out of trouble. No one expected you'd be able to take down a guy at least twice your size with a knife in the jugular."

I kept my eyes on his face, wondering at how young he looked for a detective, then let out a nervous laugh before answering his unspoken questions. "I got lucky, I think. Finding that knife there on the ground, I mean. Just wanted to get him off me and make sure he didn't hurt Marie anymore."

"How'd you know he'd taken her out there? She doesn't remember leaving the stage or walking out there with him at all."

"I didn't, really." I paused, putting my thoughts together as he pulled a small notepad from his coat pocket. "Usually, if there's a problem, the girls go to the dressing room. They can lock the door if they need to and when things are under control, they come back out."

"But that didn't happen this time?" he asked.

I shook my head. "I knew something was wrong. The dressing room was empty. The back door is right down the hall, so I thought I should check it." I paused, the silence stretching out between us.

When I didn't continue, he asked gently, "Can you tell me what you saw?"

Nodding, I closed my eyes and called my own magic into being. The warmth of it rushed through me, pulsing, too much. I reigned it in, only allowing a little to remain free, fluttering through me with the beat of my heart. I let the smallest amount of it trickle out with my words. To make him believe me. The best lies are based in truth. "He had her up against the wall in the alley. It was dark, but it looked like, maybe he was biting her or something. When he saw me, he let go of Marie and grabbed me."

I added a hint of panic to my voice at the end, a flourish in my performance. I stopped, staring down into the mug, watching the whirls of steam drift up. The scratch of a pen filled the room as Detective Bishop scribbled his notes. He gave me time to recover before he asked, "Then what happened?"

"I tried to pull away and run, but he knocked me down." I swallowed, a convulsive movement as I remembered what came next. The weight of him holding me down, his hands bruising on my skin. "I must've hit my head, because suddenly he was on top of me, his hands around my neck. I couldn't breathe, and I kept pushing up against him, but he was too big. I was trying to feel for something on the ground I could hit him with and the knife was just there. I stabbed him with it." My voice gave out. I took a shaky breath, another swallow of tea and then wiped my teary eyes with the edge of the jacket. That was it. All I had to tell.

"You're sure you'd never seen him before?" the detective asked.

I waited for a moment, like I was thinking back over all the customers I'd seen in the club. Finally nodding my head, I let a little more magic infuse my answer. "I've got a pretty good memory for faces and I don't remember him ever coming in." His shoulders slumped a little, his disappointment visible. "Would it be okay if I go home? I'm cold, and I really want to get cleaned up." I finished with another push of magic, the sweet taste of it carried along with my voice.

Detective Bishop watched me, his pupils spreading out, thin rays of silver sparking within. He closed his eyes for a moment, as if the light was suddenly too bright, shaking his head, and when he opened them again, they had returned to normal. "Those are all the questions I have for tonight. But if anything comes up, you'll hear from me. I'll have someone drive you home."

CHAPTER THREE

THE OFFICERS Detective Bishop had assigned to see me home weren't content to drop me off outside my building. They insisted on walking me inside, checking the dark corners and even the inside of my apartment before leaving me alone. They waited until I turned the locks before their footsteps moved away down the hall.

The quiet of my apartment wrapped around me, a comfort. Alone, I didn't have to worry about crowds of people, or be constantly vigilant so I wouldn't steal from them. I didn't have to fight against temptation and need, knowing the energy of those around me would be warm and so very delicious if I would just give in. Holding a shield in place any time I was around others was exhausting. Even in the interview with Detective Bishop, I'd been careful to only push the tiniest bits of magic at him. Measure by measure. I hadn't taken anything from him. And sitting behind those two young police officers he'd insisted take me home had been torture.

Hells, I was hungry.

I gulped down a stale bagel from the kitchen as I stripped off my ruined clothes. Some of the tension eased from my shoulders, the edge of my hungers eased, and I took a deep breath, letting relaxation seep into every part of me. I indulged in the hot shower I'd been imagining, scrubbing at my skin with the soap. Streaks of rust swirled around my feet before draining away. I rested my heat-soothed muscles against the wall until the shaky feeling in my stomach faded. Eventually, warm throughout, I shut the water off and stepped out, wrapping a soft towel around me. I dried quickly, not bothering with my hair. I threw on some old pajamas and collapsed into bed, sleep taking me over without a thought.

When I woke hours later, I organized my exit. I cleaned the entire apartment; every surface and corner, even inside every cabinet. There had to be nothing of me left behind, no indication I'd been there at all. When daylight started to fade, I took a few minutes to call the club's office and tell them I was too scared to come in. No one questioned my fear.

That done, I looked around the unlit apartment, the setting sun casting an orange glow over everything. A blue tarp was laid out in the center of the floor, candles holding down the four corners. I walked to the middle, dropped down with my legs crossed and sat there, closing my eyes. Everything drifted away until I was focused only on this moment. Magic rose up inside, answering my call, eager to be released. The hair on my arms stood, electricity growing, the prick of it nipping at my skin. The pure clean smell of ozone built up, and the sharp taste of metal hit my tongue. I directed my magic toward the candles, a drop for each one and smiled when they ignited. It still made me proud, calling a flame to life. Once it required all my effort. Now it came easily.

While the candles burned high, I let my magic grow, filling every part of me. When I couldn't hold any more, my skin stretched from the inside. I pushed it out away from me, directing its fury at the space around me with a simple command.

Purify.

Magic leaped forward from where I sat, rocking me back as it pulsed out from my core. The small flames of the candles wavered in its wake, their heat intensifying around me as my power fed on their thermal energy. Unleashed, it raced out. Bright blue fire scoured every surface from ceiling to floor. In my mind, I followed its course through every room, watching it find every hidden crack and even fill the pipes with its power. It burned, wiping away any remaining trace of my presence, physical or magical. When it was done, I whispered my thanks and felt the power seeping slowly away, back into the heart of me where it had taken root. A hint of a caress whispered across my back as it faded. The candles snuffed themselves out, and I was left in darkness.

I rose carefully to my feet, wrapping the candles up in the middle of the tarp. I carried the bundle under my arm and stepped out of the apartment, mouthing a soft word. The door shut securely behind me, locking itself. The keys were on the counter with an extra month's rent in payment for my abrupt departure. Everything that had made me Janey Lynde was already packed up in the car. I was out of Angel Falls. I'd call the club tomorrow morning and tell them I was too afraid to come back at all. No doubt they'd forget about me soon enough. It was time for me to go home.

Chapter Four

IT TOOK ME three days, driving back roads and changing direction, discarding the car I'd driven when I was Jane Lynde and making sure it couldn't be traced back to me. My skin began to feel comfortable again and I relaxed, the need to constantly shield myself from everyone no longer pressing down on me. Seeing the turn leading to my property peek out amid the trees made me smile against the tiredness I was beginning to feel.

I climbed out from behind the wheel of my car, and as my feet touched the ground, I knew everything was exactly the way I'd left it, nothing disturbed. The protective wards I'd activated all those weeks ago welcomed me home as I stepped past them, their power tickling over my skin and washing me in their warmth. The deep black stones that marked out the secure boundary shone wetly in the moonlight, a reassurance that no other magic had broken through. I took a deep breath of the air, the clean brisk scents another confirmation that everything was as it should be. Stars were visible above me, a fat moon bright in the night sky.

Walking in the door of my own house was a relief. In no mood to sit in the dark, I turned on all the lights as I moved from room to room. The fireplace turned on with a stab at the remote and I curled up on the couch in front of it. The music I'd turned on washed over me; the quiet notes a classical balm. Familiar scents of my own space, bergamot and spiced tea, soothed me further as I closed my eyes. It was so very good to be home.

The comfort I was feeling fled as pressure built up around me, my ears screaming to pop. As it released, a sudden rush of heat hit me from behind and a mix of pungent sulfur and musky brimstone filled the room. The scents were strong and surrounded me within seconds; a powerful presence that would linger. I didn't open my eyes, knowing what was coming.

"DELANEY ANGELIQUE MURPHY!" His voice was just as I expected, loud and angry.

"Hello Daddy," I said with a sigh as I stood up. "Let's get this over with."

Angus Murphy glared at me from a few feet away, the couch a minor barrier between us. He was still every bit the rock star who'd won the world's affection years ago, from his carefully tousled coppery curls to the ripped jeans he wore. A black leather jacket hung on his long, lean frame and his faded T-shirt peeked out as he moved. Nothing about him had changed in all the years since his plane had crashed shortly after takeoff. That's why there were still reports of Angus sightings on a regular basis in every tabloid imaginable. And right now, the rock star in front of me was furious. His long legs ate up the small distance between us almost instantly as he stepped around the couch, eyes filled with snapping flames telling me precisely how angry he was.

"What in all my Hells were you thinking? You could've been killed! Taking on a Chaos Demon? I raised you to know better than to try something like that."

"I did okay on my own," I said, trying not to sound petulant. "He's dead, I'm not. Everybody wins." Hoping to maneuver a change of subject, I gestured at him. "Guess this explains why your face has been splashed all over magazine covers lately."

"First of all, Angus sightings are proven to increase the sale of the Angus Murphy merchandise which supports you, your mother, and the charitable foundation you both love so much. Second, I fail to see how your potential death is a win for anyone, Delaney. Putting yourself in this situation without back-up." His tirade was gaining speed. "You spent weeks in that strip club waiting for him to show up and never thought to talk to me about this."

"What exactly would I have told you, Dad? That I thought a demon was hunting dancers and eating them for dinner? We both know what you would've said."

"You should've left this to me. He was mine to take care of."

"But I was able to handle it. You've had me training with Uncle Newt for years."

His voice went dangerously low, every word enunciated. "I asked Newton to work with you only so you could defend yourself if needed. Not so you'd go looking for a fight."

"I had a knife. I was ready for him."

"You had the element of surprise. That's the only reason you're still here."

"Give me some credit. I'm good at this." I stopped, aware I'd raised my voice. If I was going to convince him, it had to be by proving my plan was sound. "I was there in disguise. Costumes and wigs, too much makeup, like every other woman working there. I purified the apartment, and no one will be able to trace the car I was driving. Janey Lynde is gone. Forgotten."

My father glared at me. I was sure the stubborn set of my jaw matched his. "There's no way anything can be connected to you?"

"They have everything they need to wrap this up. No one will come looking for me."

He sank down onto the couch, and I could see the tension begin to ease from him. "I made sure there were no problems with the body. His fangs disappeared when he died so he looked human enough."

Of course he'd check on that. I sat down and rested against him. "Thank you, Dad."

I felt his laugh before I heard it. "You're devious when you want to be." I heard a hint of pride before his voice sobered again. "I know you want to prove yourself but charging in to fight demons is something else entirely. And you insist on living out here in the middle of nowhere on your own. I've tried to tell you this isn't healthy, but you won't listen."

"I like this place. It's not as if I never see anyone."

"Don't pretend with me. I know exactly why you've isolated yourself in this old farmhouse. The only thing about this demon hunting scheme that made me at all happy when I heard about it was that you were around people. You need that energy. You can't survive without it."

I sighed. He was right, but I just couldn't bring myself to steal energy from others. I'd seen the pain it caused in my own family, the grief it still caused both my parents. I refused to do that to someone else.

"I get by. You don't have to worry about me."

He put his arm around my shoulders, pulling me gently to his side as he pressed a kiss into my hair, the curls that were pure copies of his. He held me there, the warmth pouring off him and filling me up. His voice, when it came, sounded sad, a rare thing for my father. "Once I worried you couldn't have a normal life. Now you're fighting demons face to face."

I didn't want to push too hard, but I knew I had to make some things clear. "Your definition of normal and my definition have never been the same." I held my breath after those words left me, the quiet heavy in the space around us.

Angus was the one to break the silence. "Okay. I'll agree to you staying here for now." When I let out a small laugh to celebrate my win, he continued. "But you being alone isn't an option anymore, not one I can live with."

"I have Uncle Newt. I don't need anyone else."

"No. He's needed Below. Besides, you've got that old demon drummer wrapped around your finger." His emerald eyes glittered, the flames calm and low now. "I have a couple of other options in mind. Don't fight me on this."

I weighed my chances. If I wasn't willing to compromise a little, I'd likely find myself exactly where I didn't want to be, taken back to Hell, in a safe place prepared just for me. Angus had threatened as much before. Better to give a little and stay where I was.

"Okay. But no matchmaking. You're terrible at it."

I knew I'd won the round when he laughed. He pulled me into a hug and kissed the top of my head again. "Funny girl," he said with a small smile. "I'll be sending you some things soon. Be ready."

Standing up from the couch, he stepped away from me, the path Below opening at his very thought. I saw a triumphant grin flash across his face before he fell back and disappeared. I knew I'd won that argument far too easily.

"Nice job, Laney," I whispered in frustration. "You just made a deal with the Devil."

CHAPTER FIVE

DESPITE EVERYTHING, I slept well that night. By morning, I was ready to get back to my real life. I needed to catch up on things for the Murphy Foundation, buy some groceries, and get a workout in. Enough to keep me busy for a while. Grabbing a granola bar, I called in an order to the grocery store in the small town of Hazelwood and asked them to deliver it that afternoon. Then I dove into the work waiting for me.

It took a few hours, but I managed to address the most important business needs that had stacked up during my absence. I was wading through the last few emails when a rare knock sounded at my front door. A boy's voice called out, "Delivery, Ms. Murphy."

Surprised, I hurried to the door to find the grocer's son, Ernie, standing on my porch, his arms filled with bags. He grinned at me, his freckles moving up and down.

"Wow, Ernie, you made it here fast."

"Yes, Ma'am. Got my new car yesterday. Hadn't had a chance to really try it out on the highway until your order came in."

Looking behind him, I caught the flash of sun on the steel gray car in my driveway. It looked fast. "Very nice," I said appreciatively.

"Yeah, it is. Bought it with my own money. Dad said that since I'm sixteen and I've been driving for so long anyway, I could go ahead and use the money I saved up to buy the one I wanted." He winked. "I think the girls will really like it."

I laughed. He was a charmer and I was sure there were plenty of young women he enjoyed flirting with. Reaching out, I took the bags from him. "I'll put these in the kitchen. Just give me a second." I carried them in and set them on the counter, then grabbed my wallet and pulled out some cash for him. Hurrying back to the open door, I handed him the money. "For your next insurance bill."

Ernie grinned at that, but my enjoyment of his company dimmed as I saw something moving through the tall prairie grass just to the west of my front door. The odd movement of the grass made me instantly speculate that something hidden was stalking its way toward us under cover of the golden spikes. My stomach cramped at the thought of what could be out there.

I grabbed Ernie's arm as he began to step away, careful

to make sure my fingers touched only the fabric of his sleeve and not his skin. I tried to distract him, desperately offering something I never had before. "Why don't you come in the house for a minute? Tell me all about the gossip from town." It sounded silly, even to me, but I felt too exposed standing on the porch and didn't want to risk Ernie getting hurt.

"When did you get a dog, Miss Murphy?" he asked.

Confusion swamped me. "A dog? I don't have a dog."

"Then what's that?"

I followed his pointing finger and managed to make out the shape of ears peeking up through the grass in intervals before they disappeared again in an odd hopping motion. The heavy growth that always sprang up uncontrolled in the ditches swayed with the animal's movement. Ernie walked down the steps and crossed the distance to where it was struggling toward us.

"Looks like he's hurt his paw. Come here boy." Ernie picked up the small dog, whose fur was streaked with shades of brown, from honey to golden caramel and even chestnut. I got a glimpse of a thin strip of silver running down his back. "Oh, he's heavier than he looks."

As he carried the dog over to me, I briefly debated the best course of action. I could send it to town with Ernie, give him a little more money and tell him to get the dog to a vet. Or I could do what I knew was the right thing and see if I could help him. I motioned Ernie inside and he followed me into the living room, the dog's low whining urging us on. I pointed to the couch where Ernie gently laid him down. He picked up the dog's left front paw revealing the bright spot of blood staining it. I grabbed a clean cloth from the kitchen, ran it under some warm water and came back to wrap the wound with it, letting the dog rest before starting to wipe the blood away.

When we had the area clean, Ernie assured me he'd seen this sort of thing before when his dogs had gotten into fights and he could easily treat it. With a little rest and time to recover, the dog would be back on all his feet fast enough. Then I could find a home for him. It only took Ernie a half an hour and then he said he had to get back to work. He offered to pick up some dog supplies for me and drop them off later that afternoon. He ticked off a list of everything he thought a dog would need for a comfortable recovery.

"You're going to need a bed, maybe a couple so he has choices of where he wants to sleep. And food; good food, like what we feed our pups at home. A leash, so you can take him into town with you when he's all healed up. And you should think of a name for him."

I shook my head. "Why would I name him? He's only going to be here until he's better." I heard a soft whine behind me and turned to look at the dog, still resting on the couch. He looked at me with sad eyes, and I swear he started to shake a little, like he was cold. Or scared. I sighed. "Okay, Ernie. You bring back what you think I'll need to have on hand for him for a while. Then we'll see." I handed him some extra cash that I hoped would cover everything he'd mentioned and sent him on his way. He waved cheerfully to me from the front seat of his new car before racing out of my driveway, throwing gravel everywhere as he left.

I patted the dog on the head, then went back to work at my desk. Every time I glanced over, the little guy had his head down and I was pretty sure I heard snoring from time to time. At least he was comfortable.

When Ernie returned a few hours later, the dog was awake enough to lift his head and watch as the boy carried in bags of supplies.

"What is all this?" I asked, surprised at the number of things he'd brought with him.

Ernie flushed. "Well, you never know what a dog might like. I brought three different kinds of food. And sometimes when our dogs are sick, it's hard to convince them to eat, so I brought some cans of chicken too. You can put this on top of dried food and it might get him started. I figured you could use some bowls to put food and water in for him, so those are on the bottom here." Reaching into the bag, he pulled out the bowls, followed by a retractable leash, the handle a bright purple with a repeating black fleur-de-lis pattern all over it. "And I thought this looked like you. Hey, there's even bags for it. You put them in the end here." He demonstrated, flipping it over and opening the end of the handle.

"Bags? For what?" I asked, confused.

Ernie laughed. "Um, you know. So, you can pick up his messes. These are the kind my sister likes to use for her dog. They have pretty designs on them. And they're scented so you don't have to smell, well, the stuff."

I was speechless for a second and almost thought I heard something like a canine chuckle from behind me. I turned to look at the dog, but his head was down again, his eyes half closed. When I looked back at the supplies strewn out on my counter, I sighed. This was more than I'd really thought about when considering giving the poor dog a temporary home.

"Did I bring too much?" Ernie asked. He'd run his hands through his hair and it was standing up in spikes. He bit his bottom lip, something I'd seen him do before when he was nervous.

I tried to be reassuring. "Oh no, Ernie, you did fine. I was just surprised, that's all. I've never had a dog to worry about and didn't realize everything I'd need."

"Good," he said, grinning at me. "You'll like having one around. Also, I brought these beds for him. You can put one in your living room and one in your bedroom. That way, he can sleep on the floor and still be pretty comfy."

He handed one of the beds to me and I had to admit, it was soft. The brown fabric would blend in with the rest of my furniture easily. "Good choice. I just wonder if it's a lot of stuff for him to be here temporarily."

Ernie seemed to deflate a little. "You really don't think

you'll keep him? I mean, he seems so relaxed in there. I feel like he'd be the perfect sort of dog for a lady like you."

I quirked a brow at him but swallowed the question that popped into my head. I was no more than a few years older than Ernie.

I shrugged. "I really don't know. We'll see how it goes as he heals up."

Ernie nodded. "Yeah. Still, you should try to think of a name for him. Dogs always do better when they have a name. Makes them feel like they belong. Like they're home."

"Okay, we'll work on that. Let me know if you think of a good name for him or anything else we might need," I said, gesturing at the supplies he'd brought to me. "You do seem to be the expert on dog things."

He blushed. "Thanks. Oh, I almost forgot. I showed a picture of him to my mom. She said he looks like a Yorkie, only bigger than they normally are." He glanced down at his watch, then his eyes opened wide. "Shoot, I better go. Dad's waiting on me to help him back at the store. He's been busy today."

I smiled as he passed me. "Thanks for all your help today, Ernie. I wouldn't have known what to do without you being here."

He waved goodbye as he skipped down the front steps and hurried back to his car, tearing up my driveway again as he headed out. I was going to have to get it all regraveled one of these days if he kept that up.

I shut the door and it was just me with the dog. I glanced down to find him staring intently at me. He seemed very human in that moment, his head cocked to the side, studying me.

"Well, what am I going to do with you?" I asked as I sat down beside him. "At least I have food for you to eat and somewhere to sleep besides the couch." I found myself idly scratching his ears and then running my hand along the silky fur of his back. "Just remember, this is temporary. Until you're better. Then we'll find you a good home with some kids to chase around and walk you all over town."

The dog huffed in response, then laid a paw gently on my lap and waited, looking at me. I kept petting him, my hand moving on its own.

"Okay, if nothing else, you need a name. I'll see what I can come up with. And I'll put out some food and water for you. Then I've got to get back to work and you need to rest up, get healthy again."

By the end of the afternoon, I had managed to make a lot of progress with the work that needed to be done. The dog had eaten every morsel I put out, more than I'd imagined a little guy like him would have been able to. He'd even managed to hobble out to the yard and wander around, taking care of business before coming back to scratch at my back door to be let in. Then he curled up in the bed I'd laid out near the fireplace, his head resting on the edge, watching me as I began cleaning up to make dinner. As I was putting away the bags Ernie had carried everything in, I found a couple dog toys he'd included; soft plushy things that squeaked when you grabbed them. There was even a fancy new collar, royal purple to match the leash. It seemed I was now all-in as a dog owner.

I tossed the toys out into the living room, turned on some music and began cutting vegetables for stir fry. A little chicken thrown in with them and a generous helping of teriyaki sauce made for a perfect dinner for one, with leftovers for tomorrow.

As I sat down to eat, the dog trotted into the kitchen and sat down at my feet, watching each bite as it traveled from the plate to my mouth. I shook my head at him, "No, not for you. No people food. Even I know that."

He looked at me, his eyes drooping a bit and shining wetly. I was sure he was too old for puppy dog eyes, but this was a pretty good approximation. I got up and filled his bowl with more of the food Ernie had brought for him. Pointing to his dish, I sat down and said, "There's food for you in there."

The dog gave me a reproachful look, then laid down on the kitchen floor, an audible sigh escaping as he did. I laughed and continued eating my meal, purposely not looking when he dragged himself over to the food I'd poured out and begun munching on it.

I did turn around when I heard scratching behind me and was surprised to see all the food and water gone.

Grabbing my empty plate, I rinsed it in the sink and listened to the repeated scratching until I grabbed the bag of his food. The scratching stopped. When I set the bag down again, the scratching started up again. And stopped when I picked the bag up and began to dump some more in the bowl. I had the distinct feeling he was training me.

I watched him dig into the food. "I'm sure you're hungry and I don't know how long it's been since you've eaten, but don't get used to this. You keep eating like a moose, and you'll make yourself sick."

He huffed, which I took for his version of a chuckle, then went back to work wolfing down the food like he hadn't eaten at all today. I watched him for a minute, then shook my head. "How about we call you Moose for now? Ernie says you're bigger than Yorkies usually are, and you certainly eat like a moose. Will that work for you?"

He didn't answer, but when I went out to the living room and called, "Come here, Moose!" He promptly jogged on in. I was pretty sure that had as much to do with his food being gone as anything but decided to let the name stick for the time being. Whoever took him in later could change it if they wanted to, but I felt like it suited him.

I switched the music I had playing to modern country, mixed in with the good old stuff. Feeling restless and needing to work some energy out before bed, I sang along at the top of my lungs and danced around the room, my only audience the dog watching from his bed. By myself, I could sing as loud as I wanted without a worry that someone might overhear me and be drawn in by the power of my voice. After about ten songs, I felt like I could finally get some sleep. I trudged up the stairs to climb into bed, Moose following along behind me. With the light off, sleep pulled me down faster than I'd expected. I barely felt the bounce of the mattress when Moose jumped up and lay down by my feet. I was surprised at the comforting, warm feeling having him there gave me. It was nice not to be alone.

Chapter Six

WHEN I WOKE up in the morning, it was to rain pouring down and pelting the windows. Moose was on the floor, barking as the thunder sounded, his hair standing on end. As I swung my legs out from under the blankets, he turned and walked over to me, stopping to growl over his shoulder anytime there was a rumble above us. He followed me downstairs, staying close as I brewed some tea and slathered peanut butter on toast for my breakfast. I poured food into his bowl before I sat down at the table. It didn't seem fair that he should sit there and watch me eat.

I found myself talking to him in between bites. With him there, it seemed odd to be silent. My words wandered randomly, simply voicing my thoughts.

With much to get accomplished, it was best to get started. Popping the last bite into my mouth, I logged into my computer and spent the morning getting more work done. My mother was the public face of the Murphy Foundation. I'd accompanied her to events until two years ago, but the change was necessary. She smiled and waved for the camera, even though she hated it. I did the paperwork. It worked for us.

First, I approved a few grant requests that had been sent my way for review. Then, I edited a press release before approving it. Things were clicking right along, and Moose only scratched at his bowl once to remind me to fill it up for him again. By the time I was ready for a light lunch, I'd gotten through most of the work I'd needed to get done. I heated up some of the previous night's stir fry and gobbled it down.

I heard the new email alert from my computer and decided to check it before starting my workout. The message from my mother's assistant was vague, indicating that an article had been mailed to the Foundation's address. I wasn't surprised by this. We received all kinds of mail. Mostly things sent by Angus fans, homage pieces written for local papers or school projects. But this was different. This one had been sent anonymously, no return address and no note enclosed. And based on the title, it was about me.

I opened the attachment and scanned the article, surprise turning to fear. The reporter wanted to know where I was, what I was doing, and why I'd all but disappeared two years ago. The final sentence of the email, telling me that my mother would handle this with the media and that I had nothing to worry about, was meant to reassure me. My stomach twisted. Thoughts of the worst night of my life tried to push their way through the blocks I had set up. I forced myself to breathe, to relax. Remembering what made me leave the world behind wouldn't help anyone.

Once the shaking in my hands had eased, I typed a quick reply then shut down my computer. Anxious energy still shot its way through my veins needing to be released.

My workouts had been limited by necessity while I was gone. It was time for me to get back into my regular routine. Uncle Newt had taught me that it didn't matter how much muscle you had if it wasn't trained to endure the long bouts an attack might require. If trained right, my small frame could manage a heavier attacker without much trouble. My fight with the Chaos Demon had proven I could take on someone bigger than me if I was prepared and had a plan. But that wouldn't always be true. I needed to be ready for anything.

I pushed myself hard with each exercise, until the only thing I focused on was the repetition of the moves, the strain in each muscle. By the time I was finished, I was dripping sweat and the rain outside had stopped. I thought I might as well check out the acreage before getting cleaned up, as there were some things I needed to make sure were all set for winter's arrival. I'd made promises to the previous owner of the property when I bought the place that I wouldn't let things fall apart. And she was a woman you kept your promises to.

I grabbed a sweatshirt and pulled it on before heading out. Moose followed at my heels as I stretched my legs, trying to cover a lot of ground. We hit the old barn first, which I'd turned into my garage. I had a four-wheeler in there that I used for the longer trips to the wooded area that ran along the back edge of my acreage. I kept an SUV in good condition too, knowing the peril of the country roads when covered in snow or turned into slush by heavy rain. Dad's Mustang was stored in there as well. I touched the glossy red hood fondly as I walked by. I rarely drove her, but when I did, I felt like I was flying. The **ALOOF1** license plate had suited the classic convertible so well when Angus first thought of it that I'd ordered the same phrase at every renewal.

Then there was my baby, the Hellcat, its purple paint gleaming. Angus had laughed when he'd first seen it, reminding me that he'd always called me his little Hellcat when I was growing up. He questioned the color choice, feeling somehow that the purple reduced its fierceness. I'd pulled a knife from my hidden sheath and thrown it hard enough that it stuck into the wall behind him, shaving off a bare bit of stubble from his chin. I'd followed up with a quip about how I looked good in purple. He never teased me about my car again.

I whispered an apology to my car as I walked by and

grabbed the kit of tools I carried on trips like this. I wondered about Moose trying to stay with me after he'd seemed so injured yesterday, but he seemed to be walking better. I'd let him tag along and see how he did. If we needed to come back early, I could always head back out later and let him stay inside.

The two of us followed the fence line, making sure it was all in good shape. I found a couple of small holes that were easy to patch up with what I had on me. Moose and I made good progress and we'd been out almost an hour when I caught the acrid scent of something burning on the air. Moose lifted his head, nostrils flared. He'd noticed it too.

Following the odor, I turned to the west and began jogging. After another ten minutes, with the smell growing stronger and stronger, I could make out a column of smoke that had been hard to see against the gray sky when I was further away. I moved toward it, worried about what a fire back here could mean. With the rain this morning, everything was still wet. Still, I didn't want to risk flames spreading with the strong Nebraska wind.

As I broke through the trees, I could see the red flickers of a small fire jumping up. I didn't sense anyone around but I paused anyway, listening for the sound of someone moving through the woods. There was nothing to indicate danger was nearby. Picking out details of the fire ahead of me, it was obvious it was intentional. Something had been laid across the top of it, causing the harsh scent that first caught my attention. Moose growled at my side and I flinched, having forgotten he was there. Kicking loose dirt onto the flames suffocated them. When they died down, I was able to examine what had been left behind to be consumed.

The bodies were laid out next to each other, their fur charred and sightless eyes staring up at me. Moose growled again, and I ran my fingers along his back, having sunk down onto the ground, ignoring the dampness working through my pants. A fox and a rabbit, side by side, covered the wood that had been set out on top of the pyre. They hadn't been intended to be a meal, as they'd been left there to burn intact rather than skinned and skewered. Moose sniffed at the air and I tested it too, wondering what he was sensing. All I could smell was the smoke and cooked flesh. Moose began whining and pawing at the ground. Noting how methodical he was being, I realized why. He was digging a grave, giving me a place to bury the bodies.

I dug around in my pack, coming up with the work gloves I'd used when mending the fence earlier. With those on, I transferred the corpses into the hole and watched as Moose covered them up. I wondered for a moment if this was normal dog behavior. A shiver from sitting so long on the wet ground pulled me from my thoughts. It was time to get back to the house. I needed a shower to warm up and a chance to recover from the sadness and worry the scene had triggered.

On the walk home, I couldn't help glancing back. I had a

haunting feeling we were being watched but couldn't pinpoint where it was coming from. Moose never left my side, matching my speed even as I wondered how he was managing with his injured foot. He seemed to be watching the tree line to our right and his fast pace urged me on. Whatever he was sensing eluded me, but I trusted that if he was worried, I should be too. By the time the house was in sight, we were both well past walking and there was a stitch starting in my side, just above the rib I'd once had knocked out of place during a training session with Uncle Newt.

Entering the yard, I felt the ward stones test me, a tickle of electricity along my skin as they recognized that I belonged and allowed us in. I whispered the word needed to bring them back to full power as we stepped up onto the porch. The force of the energy rushing back in to fill the space behind me sucked away the air for a moment. I watched the area behind my house, searching for anything that seemed out of place. Finding nothing, I turned and went inside. It was time to get cleaned up and warm. Then I could deal with whatever might be waiting out here.

Chapter Seven

I WAITED until the water ran hot and steamy before stepping into the shower, the heat having warmed the cold tiles. I relaxed, letting the water wash away the reek of smoke and ashes, fear and death. The odor clung to me and I ached to remove it. I poured more shampoo into my hand than I really needed, wanting the comforting scents of vanilla and almonds to engulf me. I scrubbed at my hair, my fingernails roughly scratching my scalp. It was hard to feel truly clean some days. When I could no longer smell the stench I'd carried home with me, I grabbed the milk and honey soap I loved and lathered up. I breathed deeply, these familiar fragrances filling me with calm. As the tension escaped from my muscles, my shoulders relaxed back down, and I was able to breathe easy once again.

I turned off the water, opened the shower curtain, and started to reach for my towel. The pressure in the small room suddenly increased, a freezing flash of air running over my wet skin causing painful goosebumps to erupt. My ears popped forcefully, causing me to stumble, and the closed door thudded as Moose launched himself at it, his angry growling audible from his position in the hallway. I wavered on my feet, trying to regain my balance as my head spun. I closed my eyes and forced myself to breathe long and deep, letting the air fill my lungs completely before releasing it. Feeling better, I opened my eyes and yelped when I saw a man peering into the shower at me. Moose's growling increased and he battered at the door again.

"Miss Murphy?" the man asked, reaching his hand out to me.

I backed away as much as I could, but there was little room to move. There was nothing I could use as a weapon. My feet slipped on the wet tile. I had to steady myself with a hand against the wall. I stood as tall as I could, trying to infuse a confidence I didn't feel into my presence.

"Who are you?" I asked as calmly as I could. "And WHY are you in my bathroom?"

"I'm Callum," he said, as if that simple statement should answer my question. When I shook my head at him, he frowned and pointed at his chest. "Callum. Angus sent me to you."

Seeing my confusion, he kept his hands up and open, a posture that told me he wanted to appear like he wasn't a threat. I knew as well as anyone that it was easy to look like you weren't much of a threat, even if that wasn't the case at all.

"That's it? You show up in my house uninvited and I'm just supposed to believe that Angus sent you?"

The man looked directly at me, his gaze intent. His voice solemn and reverent, he said, "He wanted me to remind you, there once was a woman who unmade the Devil and their daughter played with her toys on the floors of Hell."

I stared at him, shock running through me. Angus had never felt the need to use that phrase. Our agreement was that if anyone came to me using that code, it was because Angus felt I was in danger and he was sending protection.

It also explained the disorientation that Callum's appearance in my bathroom had caused. My father could enter through the wards I had set up to protect the house, but if he wasn't actually coming through, it would have taken significantly more energy to shove an unrelated person into the gap successfully. Add to that any urgency or worry he'd been feeling at that time, and it explained why the disturbance had knocked me off balance. It must have required a lot of power. It had also gotten my dog's attention, as he tried to knock the door down again.

"It's okay, Moose. I'm fine—nothing's going to hurt me right now. Calm down," I said loudly in what I thought might be a soothing voice, hoping he'd hear me above his snarls.

I turned my attention back to the tall man standing in

front of me. "I'm sorry. You have me at a bit of a disadvantage right now. Maybe we should discuss this in a few minutes. Downstairs." I tried to make my hint as obvious as possible. Standing in my shower naked and dripping wet was no way to start a conversation with someone my father was dumping on me.

"A disadvantage?" Callum asked, his brow creasing in what I could only interpret as confusion. "I'm sorry, but I'm afraid I don't understand what you mean."

"Well, you see, I'm like this," I fumbled, gesturing vaguely at my nakedness, "and you're not."

"Oh yes. Fair enough." He smiled and there was a flash of light between us. When my vision cleared, his clothes had disappeared. I also couldn't help but notice that he'd magicked himself wet, water beading up on his skin. His long elegant fingers traced the outline of his body, emphasizing the changes he'd made at my request. "And now we're the same."

The same? By no stretch of anyone's imagination could we be described as the same. He stood there, a relaxed casual stance. His hair curled wetly around his ears and drops of water ran slowly down his shoulders and chest, carving a trail toward strong legs and—I forced myself to stop at the etched hollow of his hips. I chose to forgo modesty, using my shaking hands to cover my eyes instead of other parts of me. "Uh, that doesn't really help. I think we need to talk while we're both wearing clothes. Yeah, um, okay. Please put your clothes back on and go downstairs. I'll be there in a few minutes."

His response surprised me. "Your wish is my command." I couldn't see his face, but I could hear the grin in his words, the sound of mischief in his voice.

I waited with my hands over my eyes until I heard the door open and close. When I believed it was finally safe, I relaxed, peeking through my fingers to confirm I was alone. My bath towel was hanging in midair in front of me, easily within reach. I grabbed for it and wrapped it around me to stop the shivers that were taking over. There was no way I could mistake the laughter I could clearly hear outside the door as my unexpected guest left me alone to get dressed.

Chapter Eight

My living room seemed very small as I walked in. It felt like Callum took up a lot of space, even though he was just sitting on the couch, watching my dog watch him. Except it wasn't my dog. Instead of a largish Yorkie, there was a black horse of a canine with visible fangs crouched on the floor, his eyes never leaving my unexpected guest. Said guest had at least started the fireplace, so I tried to appreciate that act of consideration. I also noticed he didn't have his feet on my coffee table. When it feels like nothing is going quite how you want, always try to find something positive to focus on. Heat and feet on the floor were about all I had to work with. I'd make do.

"So," I said, sitting in my favorite chair across from him, uniquely positioned to allow me to see both the man and the midnight black dog on my floor. "Who exactly are you and what have you done with my dog?"

He cleared his throat, almost sounding nervous. "Again, my name is Callum, but you are welcome to call me Cal. Your father felt you might want someone to keep an eye on things, make sure you had back up if something went wrong. He thought I was a good choice."

"Let's be clear, Cal." I emphasized his name more sarcastically than I probably needed to. "I don't need your help. You can go. Free and clear, thanks for checking in." I stood up to emphasize that this was the end of the conversation, but the infuriating man stayed where he was.

He shook his head, a concerned look on his face. "Your father disagrees, and as we're both under his rule, I think you can understand that neither of us really has a choice in this matter. I'm afraid you're stuck with me, whether you want to be or not."

Rage swarmed up from my belly. I maintained my control, but my voice was tight, the words I spat out at him dangerously low. "Let's be very clear. I am not under anyone's rule. This is my life. Anyone who thinks otherwise is not welcome here." This was my life. Mine. I'd built it up from wreckage. I'd made this home, in spite of my father's legacy.

Callum lifted his hands in what I guessed was meant to be a placating gesture. "I'm sorry. But while you may be free to make your own decisions, ultimately, I am not. I am bound to your father, and therefore, I have very little choice but to follow his instructions, which, at this time, is to move myself into your spare bedroom, watch over you, and keep you safe."

I sat back down, my legs refusing to hold me up as realization hit. This was the deal I'd made last night. Angus was really doing this to me. There was no way out. Not for Callum. And certainly not for me. The words tasted bitter as they left my mouth. "Fine. If that's the way it has to be. For now." I glared at him, folding my shaking hands and hiding them in my lap.

Callum stood up and walked toward me, each step careful as he crossed the distance between us. He knelt down when he was just out of my reach and looked directly in my eyes. "Your father loves you very much. He's willing to suffer through your anger if it means you'll be safe. I'm not a bad guy and I promise I'll try very hard not to make you feel uncomfortable. But until your father says otherwise, there's really nowhere else I can go."

I understood the truth of what he was saying. Because of his connection to Angus, he really was stuck with me. The poor guy had no choice but to remain by my side, until my father said otherwise. I could choose to make us both miserable during that time or find a way we could manage to live with it.

"Okay," I said as agreeably as I could manage. "Then the least you can do is tell me what you did to my dog. And why this thing is here with you." I pointed at the enormous black shadow that was slinking away to the dog bed by the fireplace and snapped my fingers. "Hey, that's not for you!"

Cal's hand on my arm stopped me. "I'm sorry, Miss Delaney. I thought you knew you had a Hound living here with you."

"A Hound?" I asked, confused. "I don't have a Hound. I have a Yorkie." I waved my hand at the enormous canine draped across a bed that was ridiculously small. His legs stuck out awkwardly. But his eyes watched me a little sadly and he rested his head on his front paws, ears down, dejected.

"Yes, a Hell Hound. He picked an appearance he thought you'd like at first, but he can change shape and size as needed. He's quite communicative. Also, he doesn't mind that your father sent him here. He appreciates the way you've made him comfortable. And he likes the name you've given him very much."

I gaped at him as I processed the information. Finally, something clicked. "You can talk to him?"

Cal shrugged. "I've been around Hounds a lot. One learns how to listen."

I looked over at Moose, not sure what I could or should do in this moment. He raised his head and blinked at me, then laid back down as if there was nothing really to say.

"Is there anything else I should know about? Anything else my dog has said to you?" I asked, making no effort to hide my caustic tone.

Which Cal chose to ignore.

"Oh yes. Your Hound and I have come to an agreement, you could say. I have promised not to hurt you and he has promised not to eat me."

I rested my head in my hands for a moment while I absorbed this information. A conspiracy. Even the damn dog was in on it. When Daddy Dearest decided to invade my life, he did it in every way he could possibly think of.

This was all enough for one night. I stressed the point that we were done by standing up to lead the way out of the room. "I'll show you where you will be sleeping. Do you have anything that you need to get? Extra clothes maybe?"

He shook his head and followed me up the stairs. "I can do that tomorrow. I'll be fine for tonight. We can both get some sleep and talk more about this arrangement in the morning."

"But don't you need something to sleep in?" I asked as I opened the door to the spare bedroom and pulled clean sheets out of the top dresser drawer.

He stepped forward and took the linens from me. "No," he said, bending over the bed and stretching the fitted sheet over the mattress. "I prefer to sleep with nothing on." He glanced back at me, a wicked grin on his face.

I bit my tongue as I rushed out of the room, tasting blood as I slammed the door on his accompanying laughter.

CHAPTER NINE

WHEN I WOKE the next morning, it was to the sounds of someone downstairs in my kitchen. I could hear pans rattling, a man's voice carrying up the stairs, and the occasional bark of my dog. Everything from the night before hit me again.

I pulled the pillow over my head and tried to wish it all away. It didn't work. I needed to face the day and the problem before me. I pulled on what were possibly a clean pair of sweatpants and T-shirt, finger combed my hair, and stepped into my bathroom to brush my teeth. The woman I saw in the mirror looked tired, the shadows under her green eyes emphasized by the paleness of her skin. "You can do this," I told her. "You can manage one man living in your house. Hells, you've killed a demon on your own. You can handle this."

Pep talk done, I clenched my teeth and headed downstairs. To the man waiting for me.

"Good morning," Callum said as I walked into the kitchen. I held my hand up in front of me, shading my eyes from the bright light streaming through the windows. "I thought it might be helpful if I made breakfast for us this morning. We'll probably need the energy as we hash out this arrangement." He sounded so certain and pleasant. The smell of coffee hung on the air and I savored it. It was one of my favorite scents even though I thought the beverage itself tasted like someone poured a disgusting mix of water and dirt into a cup.

"I'm not much of a morning person," I said in response, grabbing what I needed to make my daily dose of tea. "I don't usually eat breakfast and I don't drink coffee." Callum's smile faded at my words and I realized he'd likely been working on this for a while. "But, everything smells delicious," I added. This seemed to brighten his expression some, so I continued on as cheerfully as I could manage. "And you're probably right. We've got a lot to get through today and we'll need energy to do that."

Callum seemed to sense that my mood wasn't inclined toward conversation. He finished making breakfast quietly, finding plates and filling them with scrambled eggs and bacon. Toast popped up and filled the air with its warm scent. When I felt more in control of my emotions, I turned toward the table, grabbing napkins along the way. I sat down across from Cal and we both began to dig in, eating silently for a few minutes.

I was the first to break. "I don't mean to take my anger out on you. I know you don't have any choice in this mess, but I'm not used to having to share this space with anyone. I've always been independent. It's hard to hear that my father doesn't have faith in me."

Callum sipped at his coffee, his eyes focused on me as I spoke. As I finished, he said, "It's not that he doesn't have faith in you. He worries about you—constantly." He paused, like he was searching for the right words, before continuing. "He knows you have this need to make the world better. He thinks you're convinced the only way you can do that is if you take on all the evil you find and destroy it. That makes him afraid you'll put yourself in harm's way. That you'll sacrifice yourself if you have to."

I couldn't argue with that. "Anything else you know about me?"

He stared at his plate, quiet for a moment. "I know you live out here alone, because you're afraid that if anyone gets too close to you, they could be hurt. From what Angus said, you've inherited his talents, but they didn't appear until you were older. Sixteen?"

I caught my breath. That was something Dad and I rarely talked about. Uncle Newt and my mother were the only ones who knew the whole truth of how my powers had manifested. Of the damage I'd been able to do. I sipped my tea to buy a little time. If Angus had told this secret to Callum, then it meant he trusted him. I might as well give it a shot. "I don't talk about this with anyone."

Callum didn't say anything—just sat there listening.

"Everything was fine. I was exactly like everyone else, growing up. And then, one night I changed."

I stopped there, not wanting to continue.

Cal's voice was gentle this time, the teasing and banter he'd used before gone. "You can't prepare for something you don't know is coming." His words were genuine, heavy with some feeling I couldn't identify fully. He locked eyes with me. "I understand. More than you think I do. I know how it feels to want to change things, knowing you can't."

I laughed, a brittle sound cracking through the air. I'd thought of that one moment too many times. It was a wound I kept tearing open, wondering if things might have been different if I'd only walked a different way. Not said yes. Not tried to be a normal girl. Of all the things my father could do, the magic he'd taught me to work, turning back time wasn't a trick either one of us knew. No matter how much we wished we could. I tore the toast in my hands into tiny pieces, watching them drop onto my plate. My stomach twisted at the idea of eating any more. "So, two years Below. That's how much time I spent there. Learning. Practicing. Hoping I wouldn't hurt anyone else. Finally, I decided it was time to leave." There was a pain in my voice that surprised me. "Angus wanted me to stay with him. Bargained with me. But in the end, he let me go."

Callum stood up, clearing away the plates, his distance

giving me a moment to compose myself. Standing at the sink, rinsing dishes off, he said, "Not many people survive two years Below, Laney. At least, not intact." Again, there was a current of understanding that passed between us, as if he'd lived something similar.

I nodded, even though I knew he wouldn't see me. I took a drink of my tea, the strong familiar scent of Earl Grey comforting. Time for a change of subject. "How did you make coffee? I don't even have anything to make it with."

He laughed. "Moose helped me with that. We hopped out to my place while you were still sleeping, and I was able to grab a few things—toothbrush, a coffeemaker, and my favorite roasted blend."

"How exactly did my dog help you with that?"

"Well, since you've made him yours, he's tied here. He was able to anchor me and connect your home with mine for a short time. Long enough that I was able to get the essentials. I don't do well without my coffee in the morning."

"I didn't realize he could do something like that. Or that he was *mine*. But then, I also thought he was just a dog." I made sure to shoot a pointed look at Moose, who completely ignored me. He was curled up in his bed, nose tucked in and eyes closed.

Callum smiled at that silent exchange and leaned on the granite top of the island. "If you're willing, you could come with me to get the rest of my things. I can show you how to open that road, so you'll know how to do it in an emergency."

I shrugged and sipped my tea, thinking about it. It wasn't a bad idea and it was a skill that could be helpful in the future. "Okay. But give me a little more time to wake up. It's still too early for something like that."

Leaving Callum to finish cleaning up the kitchen, I went back to my room to put on real clothes. It's always easier to face the day when you feel like you look somewhat decent, so I took a few minutes to wash my face and then smeared some lip balm on. By the time I had pulled my hair back and secured it with a few pins to keep it out of my eyes, I felt like I could do this.

Back downstairs, the kitchen was shiny, and the dishwasher was humming away. He must have used some super speed to do all this because I really hadn't been gone very long. I found him riffling through my large pantry, some large white garbage bags in his hands.

He glanced at me and waved the crinkly plastic at me. "The luggage of the most worldly travelers. You don't mind?"

Shaking my head, I asked, "Why didn't Angus help you bring stuff with you when he sent you here?"

Callum shrugged. "It took a lot for him to send me through. He had to get back Below right away to handle something, but he didn't want to wait to send you some back-up. Opening your wards and shoving me through left him with enough energy to take care of business. That's all I know."

The rush of frozen air when he'd appeared the night

before came back to me. "Wherever you were when he sent you to me must have been cold."

He laughed. "I was hiding in the walk-in freezer of my restaurant. Thought the cold might keep him from sensing me."

That bit of information was a little bit concerning. "Why were you hiding?" I asked him, trying for innocent curiosity.

He winked at me. "If you're smart, you always hide from the Devil when you know he's looking for you." He handed me the bags and asked, "Ready to go?"

"As I'll ever be."

CHAPTER TEN

I TRIED TO hide my fascination, but it was hard. Callum rested one of his warm hands on my arm as he held the other out in front of him. When he spoke, his voice was firm. "Open."

The air surrounding us rushed forward, and the few strands of hair I'd missed blew into my eyes. A tunnel opened in front of us. I felt the charge of magic prick at my skin as we stepped forward, Cal's hold on me tight. As we walked, he whispered to me. "Remember this. Each place has a feeling to it that is unique, something you connect to. It can be a picture in your mind, a scent, a desire. Whatever works for you. Just make it distinct in your mind and focus on it when you want to find your way there."

I nodded, recognizing the practical importance of this learning opportunity. Any time you have the chance to watch someone work magic and they're willing to share their secrets, it's best to remember every detail you can.

Stepping out of the windy tunnel, I was surprised by Callum's apartment. The exposed brick reminded me of some historical buildings I'd seen before, and the furniture was the kind that made you want to sit and stay a while. He saw me trying to take everything in and grinned.

"I know you like music. Why don't you look through the vinyl I have over there and see if there's anything you want to take with us. I can load up the system and get everything put together at your house when we have a few minutes."

I wandered to the stacks of albums he pointed out and began sorting through them. I recognized a lot of old blues albums, the crossroads songs catching my attention. The variety of music he'd collected intrigued me—even bluegrass and some head banger metal I wouldn't have dreamed he'd appreciate. I set a few aside that I thought we might both enjoy and then followed him into his bedroom. He was laying out clothes to take on the gray silk coverlet over his king size bed. I glanced around the room, noticing that the walls were a dark blue that managed to feel warm instead of inspiring a chill. Everything in the room was welcoming.

"Is there anything I can help you find or pack up?" I asked, feeling like I should do something besides prowl around his home and use it to dissect him.

"Not really. I don't need a lot of stuff. Clean clothes, some music, maybe a few movies, and some books I've been wanting to read."

"I don't think you'll be staying very long," I said, trying to make him feel better about our situation.

"Oh really. Can't wait to get rid of me already?"

"It's not that. But I can imagine it would be hard to be told you have to abandon your life for an unknown length of time and have no choice in the matter."

He nodded over his shoulder at me before turning back to his clothes. "It's not easy to be told what to do. The trick to dealing with it is to find the good in the situation you're being pushed into."

I snorted at that. "What good is there in this situation?"

He looked at me. "I met you. That's a good thing."

I stared at him surprised until I registered that he was staring right back, waiting for me to say something. "Um, yeah. You too."

He laughed. "Well, that was awkward. But I appreciate the effort."

I couldn't help but smile back, his good humor infecting me little by little. "You sure there's nothing else I can do?"

Slipping the last few pieces of clothing into the bag, he shook his head. "I think we can go. If you want to pack up the albums you chose and the books I have out on the counter, I'll get this stuff."

Doing as he asked, I loaded the music into an empty bag, then piled the books in carefully. "Are you sure? We can always come back later for more."

"Careful, or I'll think you're inviting me to move in permanently."

I appreciated the joke, recognizing his attempt to lighten the mood. Joining him in the middle of the room, he had me wrap my hand around his muscled bicep and then waited while I tried to call up the pathway back to my house. I bit my lip, focused my effort stubbornly on the fact that I wanted to be back in my own kitchen, and called for the tunnel to open before us. I tried to hide my surprise when it appeared right away. As the air swirled over and around us, we walked forward together.

CHAPTER ELEVEN

MOOSE WAS UNDOUBTEDLY happy to see us, his stubbed tail twitching back and forth excitedly as he jumped up in greeting.

Cal smiled. "Thank you, Hound." His voice felt formal as he spoke to my dog. "I'll put my things away upstairs and then we'll play. Agreed?"

Moose gave a short bark that sounded happy and stepped out of the way so Callum could pass him. I settled into a chair, setting the bag I'd carried back with us on the table. Moose quirked his ears at me, a curious look on his face. I did my best to answer his unspoken question. "Opening portals, check. Uncle Newt will be proud of that one."

He walked to my side and licked my hand, like he was as happy with my accomplishment as I was. I looked into his sincere dog eyes. "I know Cal said he could talk to you.

Promise me you won't mention that little karaoke session the other night, and I'll forgive you for not letting me know you're really a Hell Hound."

Moose sat back on his haunches, head cocked to the side as if he was considering my words. With a small sigh, he stretched out fully on the ground, his nose brushing the tops of my shoes before he rested his head on them. Then he looked back up at me, waiting.

"I'll take that as an agreement."

He hopped up from his submissive pose and bobbed his head up and down, then proceeded to his food bowl. I was forgotten again as he crunched away at the kibble.

A few minutes to myself, I idly pulled the books from the bag in front of me. I swallowed my shock with a grin as I saw the titles and vivid colors on the covers. Romances. I couldn't hold back my laughter. This wasn't what I would have expected Cal to be reading. If anyone had asked, I would have guessed he probably read biographies or history books. Never romance novels.

Shaking my head, I returned to my meandering thoughts. Thoughts about my father and his reasons for throwing us all together. I tried to puzzle out exactly why he felt a dog and a guy I'd never met would be able to protect me from whatever he feared was lurking outside my door. From all the stories I'd heard of Hell Hounds in the past, they were strong, fast, and deadly when they needed to be. And the way he'd tried to take down the door when Callum suddenly appeared in my bathroom the previous night had proven he was willing to do whatever he could to keep me safe. That made sense.

But Cal I didn't understand. He'd hidden when Angus had come looking for him. His home had been clean and comfortable. He could cook. And apparently, he read a lot of romance novels. I'd seen little that would seem to indicate he was a big scary guy with magical abilities that could protect me, although the fact that he had opened a portal between his home and mine so easily was impressive. Why had my father wanted *him* here? Everything pointed to me not having enough information to see the answer. I doubted that Angus was going to be willing to answer my questions anytime soon. Moose, Callum, and I were an unlikely trio, and there was nothing to explain why we'd been thrown together.

When Cal came back downstairs, I was waiting with a fresh cup of coffee for him. As he took it from me, he seemed to read the questions on my face and sighed. "So, we need to have a talk, don't we?"

"Please."

He sat at the table while I waited by the counter. He sipped his coffee before looking back to me. "What do you want to know?"

"I want to know about you. What you are? And why Angus would send you here?"

He stared into his cup for a moment that seemed to

draw out longer and longer. Eventually, he raised his eyes and pinned me with his gaze. "Are you afraid to sit over here with me?"

I walked to the table and pulled out a chair across from him, sliding down into it, never taking my eyes from his. "Tell me."

He nodded and opened his mouth to say something but was interrupted by a knock at my front door. I glanced toward the sound then back at Callum. His face was closed, empty of emotion and the animation I'd already come to associate with him. Instead, he was on guard, alert. Moose was at attention as well, a quiet growl vibrating the air around him. There was a louder, more demanding knock as I pushed myself away from the table. Before I left to answer the door, I told Cal, "We will have this talk." I expected a response, but instead he just stood up to follow me as I moved to the front door.

There was a third knock, proof that whoever was standing outside wasn't going anywhere. And that they were strictly human, no magic in them for the wards to react to. Reaching for the handle, I was aware that both Moose and Callum had arranged themselves protectively around me. I opened the door to a tall man, his fist raised to knock again. Dark hair curled around a tanned face with the faint shadow of stubble, his eyes hidden by the dark lenses of his sunglasses. At my appearance, he smiled slightly, tiny lines forming at the edge of his lips. I stopped breathing for a moment, knowing exactly who was at my door. This couldn't be good.

"Miss Murphy? Detective Torren Bishop. Would you mind if I came inside?" He started to step forward over the threshold but froze as a loud growl erupted from behind me.

I hesitated. Then I realized I'd have to play this game, for a while at least. "I'd like to see your badge, please." I wasn't happy to have this detective at my door, but it would be suspicious if I didn't at least talk to him.

"Of course," he said. "It's right here, inside my jacket. If it's all right with you and your dog, I'm going to pull it out."

I nodded, very aware of the various muscles tensing behind me.

He moved carefully, deliberately pulling his badge out and opening it for me to see. I reviewed it, and the picture printed on it matched what I could see of him. He pulled off his glasses as I looked at his face, showing me the same bright blue eyes that stared out from his badge. Everything looked the way it should.

I opened the door wider and stepped back, only then recognizing I'd been using the door to block half of my body; that I'd been peering around it. "Come in," I said. "I've got just a little bit of time right now."

He followed me inside and then stopped when he caught sight of Callum, standing in a dark corner, at an angle to the door. If the detective had tried to do anything when I turned my back to him, Callum would have been in the perfect position to intercept him. That was obvious to me, and apparently to Detective Bishop as well.

When I was sure the situation had been clearly communicated to all parties, I nodded my head toward the couches to our right. This man wasn't getting any further into my home than I had to let him. I'd be polite, but I had my limits. Until I knew what he wanted from me, I wasn't about to give anything away by trying to guess.

I sat down and Callum perched himself on the arm of the couch I'd chosen. Moose curled up by my feet, a position that seemed relaxed, but I could tell he was on guard.

As the detective took a seat across from me, I asked, "So, what was it that you wanted to talk with me about?"

He pulled a notebook and some papers out of the inside pocket of his jacket. He opened the notebook and slid a picture into his hand, laying it down on the table between us. It was clear he wanted me to reach for it, but I stayed where I was. He smiled at me, pushing the picture closer to me until the weight of it balanced on the edge, threatening to tip off. "I wondered if you might recognize this young lady."

I looked down at the picture about to spill onto my floor and saw my own face looking back at me.

Chapter Twelve

THERE WAS NO denying that was my face, topped by a curly blond wig. The image was grainy, obviously pulled from some surveillance cameras back in Angel Falls. And that was my body barely covered by a red sequined corset and tiny shorts. Pretending it wasn't me was pointless. But I did it anyway.

"I'm afraid I don't know her. I hope she's okay?"

He laughed harshly, shaking his head. "She looks just fine to me," he said with a pointed look at my face.

I fought the anxiety clawing at my insides, forcing it down so it wouldn't show. "I don't understand. If she's all right and nothing's happened to her, why are you trying to find her? And why here, of all places?"

He shifted slightly, angling himself like he was ready to jump from his seat if needed. "Ms. Murphy, you need to understand something. I already know the answers to a lot of the questions I came here with so lying to me will do no good. For example, I know the woman in that picture is you. I know you were working in the bar when that dancer was attacked, and I know you killed the man who attacked her."

"If you think you know so much, why are you here talking to me then?" I asked before I could stop myself.

"Because I don't know everything yet. And neither do you." His bright eyes locked with mine and a current zipped between us. I knew he'd already surveyed everything, especially the way that Callum and Moose had protectively arranged themselves around me. Silence reigned for a long moment, broken only when Cal cleared his throat out of politeness.

This time, when the detective spoke, his voice was softer, almost like he was trying to ease the coming blow. "Delaney, we don't have time to lie to each other, so let's stop pretending and just be honest." He tapped the face in the picture before me with his fingernail. "This is you. I know it's you. What I don't know is why you were there."

I was perfectly still, trying to reason everything out. He'd found me, figured out who I was. He also had a suspicion that I'd been working in the club for a specific reason. Angus was going to kill me.

"You're right. This is me." My fingers traced the lines of my face briefly before I looked back up at him. "I was there because I thought someone might try to attack one of the girls. I wanted to prevent that if I could."

He looked surprised for a moment but then smiled, a real smile this time that lightly creased the skin around his eyes and made them shine a little. "But how did you know?" he asked.

"I saw a pattern, reports of women being attacked at similar clubs over the past nine months. I traced the path of attacks and Angel Falls seemed to be the most likely place for him to go next. So, I went there."

"You just went there? By yourself? To confront someone you believed had murdered other women?" he asked, disbelief coating his words.

I didn't let my frustration show. Always underestimated. "Yes, I went there by myself. I wanted to stop him. Keep him from hurting anyone else."

"How?" he asked.

"I do know how to take care of myself, believe it or not. I've been trained in self-defense. Just in case something ever happened. I used that when I had to. And I'm glad I did." I knew I sounded defensive, but I couldn't spare the energy needed to keep it from coloring my voice.

"Knowing self-defense doesn't mean you go looking for trouble. Why didn't you call law enforcement, tell them what you'd found?"

I shook my head, a brief laugh at his suggestion. "How exactly would that have turned out, do you think, Detective? The crazy, hermit daughter of a dead rock star calls and tells police that she's found a disturbing pattern of dead women and knows where the murderer will strike next. You really think that would have been taken seriously? It would have made all the gossip shows, headlined in the tabloids, but that's about it. Nobody who could do anything about it would've listened."

His eyes tracked every movement I made, his gaze making me aware of the heat growing under my skin. I looked at Callum, but he didn't look back at me. He was staring fixedly at the detective and I understood from the fierceness in his eyes that there was a strong possibility this meeting was about to go very wrong. The kind of wrong that ended with another hole dug somewhere on my property.

Hoping to reduce the tension without admitting to any more than I already had, I nodded once. "I'd like to finish this up. Do you have any other questions?"

He picked up his notebook and looked down at it briefly, then directly back at me. "So you decided that posing as a waitress named Janey Lynde would let you infiltrate the club and be there when the attack came?"

"It seemed like a good idea at the time. Gave me a legitimate reason to be there when the murderer showed up," I answered.

"Why not pose as a dancer? All his previous victims had been dancers."

"I could pull off the waitress act much better than dancer."

"But you would have been on stage, bait for the guy you

were trying to track down. You being a dancer would've made more sense than waiting on the fringes for something to happen."

I felt a wave of cold as his words hit me. If you looked at things that way, I had let another woman be victimized. I'd left her as bait for a killer while I hovered on the outside, fairly protected by anonymity. From that perspective, I was responsible for Marie being the victim, for her being hurt. I was speechless for a moment as guilt overwhelmed me.

But then reason interjected itself.

I leaned forward, unafraid to let my anger show now. "Becoming a dancer was no guarantee. You never know, maybe the owner doesn't like short women that look like me. Waitress was a job I was much more likely to get. And being on the fringes made it easier for me to watch out for anything that might happen. In fact, I spotted the guy before he got Marie out of the club and would have gotten to him if some damn idiot hadn't pulled my tail."

Detective Bishop was trying very hard not to laugh at my impassioned statements. I was absolutely sure at this point he'd seen the security footage of me falling backward, into the lap of the customer who'd tried to take advantage of the moment before I regained my feet. His time was up.

"You know, I think you can get everything else you need to know from the statement I gave back in Angel Falls."

He leaned back. "I went over that statement, again and

again, believe me. Couldn't help myself. Especially after you left town."

"Then why are you here?" I ground these words out, desperation starting to make its way into my voice.

"At first, it made sense. Then I saw your apartment. It was extremely clean, almost like no one had ever lived in it."

I shrugged at that observation. "I know how to clean really well. My parents taught me those types of things. What's that got to do with anything?"

He nodded, his sharp eyes never leaving me. "Nothing necessarily." He paused and shrugged, setting his notebook on the table. "But then I followed the money."

I froze, swallowed against the nausea that threatened to overcome me. "What money?" I asked, even as I fought the sinking feeling in my stomach.

"Your paycheck. Or should I say, the paycheck for Janey Lynde. Direct deposited into an account in her name, that then automatically dumped the money into a separate account. Into an account for a shelter that helps victims of domestic violence." He looked at his notes, even though I was sure he didn't need to refer to them at all. "Hope House. Founded and supported by the Murphy Foundation. The shelter is run by a very nice woman named Alice Cheney, who was very proud that Delaney Murphy and her mother came to the shelter once and presented a service award to her. She especially appreciated it when they both agreed to take a picture with her to commemorate the occasion. She keeps it on her desk, loves to share it with everyone who comes to visit."

My throat was dry, but I managed to get the words out. "How? How did you . . .?"

Detective Bishop shrugged, his eyes never leaving mine. "Sometimes it's not what you know, it's who you know." He waited, but when I remained silent, he continued. "Imagine how interested I was to find that the woman she pointed to in the picture and consistently referred to as Delaney Murphy looked very much like a young lady calling herself Janey Lynde from Des Plaines, Illinois."

I shut my eyes. Here it was. The one factor I didn't consider when planning everything. It seemed like such a simple thing. I would hunt down the murderer and the shelter would get a little extra money. An easy win-win. All of it ruined by a money trail and a single picture someone had taken years ago. Right before everything had changed. I'd asked her not to post it online. I'd never said anything about not displaying it in her office. My father would be so disappointed. There was nothing to do now but admit it.

I looked squarely at the detective. "So, you figured it out. Congratulations. Now, if you don't have any other questions for me, I think it's time for you to go." I stood up to walk to the door, hoping that would encourage him to follow me.

He stayed seated, even leaning back against the cushions like he was making himself comfortable. "I do have a few more questions for you, Ms. Murphy? Would you mind?"

he asked, pointing to the seat I'd just vacated.

I refused. "I'm happy to stand. Two more questions, then it's time for you to go."

He nodded, back to business. "I'm curious about the knife. It seemed too nice to have just been laying in that alley, waiting for you to need it. But looking at what you were wearing on the night the incident occurred, I couldn't see anyplace you might have hidden it that wouldn't have been noticeable."

I couldn't miss the tension that layered the question. Self-defense or armed with intent? He didn't need to know about the custom sheath built into the boots I'd been wearing that night. Designed to hold a blessed blade. I'd hated leaving my knife behind, but it would have raised too many questions if it had disappeared when I did. I played it off. "Sometimes," I shrugged, "you just get lucky." Maybe it was that I was nervous, but I realized too late that I'd coated that last word with my magic.

Detective Bishop watched me, thoughtfully, but I couldn't ignore the way his eyes dilated as they followed every move I made. "So, you went there, intending to stop him, completely unarmed?"

"I knew I'd take some hits, but I believed I could stop him somehow. That's what I did."

He seemed stunned by this information, but I ignored that, waving my hand toward the door. "Now, I've answered your questions as agreed. It's time for you to leave."

"But, what about . . . ." he started to say.

I stopped him with a quick gesture. "No. Your time is up." I walked to the door and opened it for him, making it clear that I was done answering his questions.

He stood up slowly, watching me wait at the door. When it was clear I wasn't going to change my mind, he nodded a quick goodbye in Cal's direction. As he walked toward me, I couldn't help but notice his broad shoulders and rolling gait, reminding me of a young John Wayne stalking his way through countless movies. The detective smiled genuinely at me in a way that made his eyes look even brighter in the light of the open door. He stopped and took my hand, shaking it. The fact that I didn't react in time to avoid the skin to skin contact was proof of how much he'd thrown me by coming to my home. The current I'd felt before intensified between us when his fingers touched mine. It felt like gravity was tugging at us both. I resisted the urge to close the distance.

"I know you won't believe this, Miss Murphy, but it's been a pleasure seeing you again." Then he leaned in toward me, so near I could smell the soap he'd used earlier in the day. "And for the record, I happen to like short girls who look like you," he whispered into my ear. I bit my lip as goosebumps broke out on my skin and he grinned at my response. With one last, true smile, he walked out my door. He left without looking back and I hoped to all the Hells I would never see him again.

Chapter Thirteen

I FELT A LITTLE defeated after he left. I sat in silence for a few minutes, my head in my hands, trying to come to terms with how this man had tracked me down. When I'd finished with what my mother would have no doubt called my very own pity party, I sighed and raised my head, realizing too late that I'd been watched through it all.

Callum's attempt at a reassuring smile looked more like a grimace. "You know, Angus will not be happy about all this."

I nodded. I didn't need to say anything. I'd left that loose end behind. It was a mistake. I hadn't ever expected anyone would wonder about Jane Lynde enough to even think about the money. They shouldn't have. But Detective Bishop had. He'd followed the trail, which led him right to my door.

"What's done is done," Cal continued. "We'll make the best of things as they are. You answered his questions and we'll put it all behind us for now. Let's do something you really want to do. So—you pick. What do you want to do?"

I tried to smile, but I knew it had to look almost feral. "You don't want to know what I want to do right now." I shook my head, trying to warn him away as I stood up from the couch, rolling my head to loosen the muscles that had tightened up in my neck and shoulders.

"Come on," he persisted. "We'll do whatever you choose."

I gave him a harsh laugh. "Fine. It's your funeral. Follow me."

I stalked out of the living room and showed him the hidden stairs to my basement. He followed me down and began to chuckle when I turned on the light. My entire basement had been converted into a space any fighter would love to train in. There were a couple heavy bags hanging in one corner and weights were off on another side. Everything I could need to work off my anger was right here. I pulled on the clean workout gear I kept in the bathroom. Stepping back out into the space, I found Callum had thrown off his shirt and grabbed a pair of the shorts Newt kept down here. They were slightly too big for him and hung loosely around his hips, emphasizing things that would only be a distraction.

He tried to lighten my mood with a joke. "Here I thought you were leading me down into your dungeon so you could take advantage of me. But you want to work out?"

I reached over and tied the drawstring extra tight, knotting it for him. No gear malfunctions allowed. "What I want to do right now is hit something. Hard. I'm going to start jumping rope to warm up. Do what you want, but that guy is mine." I pointed to the middle where a figure stood. "That's Bob. He takes all the abuse I can dish out."

He nodded, understanding my point. I turned some music on, loud rock pulsing through the air and got to work. After we were both warmed up and shining with a thin sheen of sweat, Callum joined me and we threw heavy medicine balls at each other. Twisting to toss and catching them, faster and faster, a competition to see who would give first. He did. He threw it down onto the padded floor, then grabbed the pads from where I'd stored them last. He motioned to the middle of the room and said, "Okay. Let's see what you can do."

We were both dripping by then, hot and flushed despite the natural underground chill in the air. I grabbed my gloves, pulling them on and tightening them with my teeth. No wraps today. It was time to pound away at the fear that I'd screwed everything up. I needed to knock down the guilt trying to sink its teeth into me.

We lined up across from each other and Callum dipped his head at me one time. "Begin," he said. I came at him immediately, jabbing with my left a few times before throwing in a right cross at his head. He caught it with the pads and then swiped at my head. I ducked down, popping back up when he was off balance and letting my upward momentum add to the power of the uppercut I aimed at his chin. He jumped back at the last moment and we circled each other for a few seconds as he caught his breath.

"Not bad," he said. "Looks like Newton has been teaching you a few things."

"Not bad?" I asked. "That's all you can say?"

He cocked his head and said mischievously, "Time for Round Two."

This time, I didn't hold back. I threw every punch I'd learned at him, even a couple elbows when he'd spun around to get behind me. I added in some heavy knees and a roundhouse kick from time to time to keep him off balance. After ten rounds of this, we were both spent. And laughing. Gut deep laughter rolled out of us until I collapsed onto the floor and felt relaxation sweep through me. After we'd calmed down, Callum helped me up.

"What's over there?" he asked as I used a towel to wipe some of the sweat off my face.

I followed his gesture and grinned. "That's where I've been practicing my knife skills. I can throw them from a decent distance, but Newt's also made me do a lot of up-close practice. There's also a nice gun range he set up for me in the tunnel back there, so I can keep working on my marksmanship."

"Wow. I would tell you I'm surprised, but knowing Newton, I'm really not."

"Oh, you know Uncle Newt? For how long?" I tried to keep my voice casual, so he wouldn't guess how much I wanted to know the answer to that question.

"Long enough to know not to mess with your father or his best friend." Then he forced a sudden subject change. "You know, when you said you wanted to hit something, I wasn't sure what to think. But this works for me."

I looked at him over my shoulder as I led the way upstairs. "Trust me, hitting things always makes you feel better. Guaranteed."

Moose was waiting for us in the kitchen, curled up in his bed, one eye open. Callum leaned down to him and whispered, "I'm going for a run and I bet you want to join me." Moose was up immediately, stretching as he did so, his snout elongating and legs growing inch after inch until his ears were at my elbow. He leaned his new weight into my side, forcing me to struggle to maintain my balance. He looked up at me and I rubbed my hands through the silky fur along the top of his spine.

"Do you want to come with us?" Callum asked, making his way to the back door with Moose right behind him.

I hate to run. "You guys go ahead without me. I'll clean up and by the time you're back, we'll all be ready for some food."

Moose dashed out the door Callum held open for him and I watched them lope off together. From where I stood on the back steps, I watched as they raced each other. Moose was mine, as Cal had pointed out, and could pass through the wards just as I could. Cal's hand was just barely visible, resting on my Hound's head as they passed the small stones that marked the boundary of my wards. Moose was a black streak next to Cal and they were out of sight all too quickly. Sighing almost happily, I jogged up to my bathroom, stripped off my soaked clothes, and turned the shower on as cold as I could stand. I stepped in, letting the water rush over me, spraying off the sweat and grime that wanted to cling to me. There would be sore muscles tomorrow, but it would feel good. Alive.

When I felt clean again, I turned the water off, wrapping a soft towel around me. The little luxuries of my life comforted me, and I let go of the remaining frustration I'd held on to. My day hadn't started as planned, but it could only get better. With a clear mind, I could figure out a way to calmly explain the situation to Angus and reassure him that there really was nothing to worry about. I could do this. I had to do this. If I didn't, I'd end up exactly where I didn't want to be. Back in my very own bedroom in Hell. Knowing Angus and his love of torture, there would be a lot of pink this time. And bows. Probably a bed with a canopy.

The phone rang, distracting me from the plans I was trying to put together.

When I answered it, my heart stopped for a second.

"Ms. Murphy, I need to meet with you one more time. There's something we need to talk about."

"I don't think so, Detective Bishop. We've talked enough already."

"You don't understand. It's very important or I wouldn't bother you at all."

"I don't want you here at my house."

"That's fine—you can come to me. I'll meet you at the coffee shop down the street from my hotel." He gave me the address and time to meet him, then hung up before I could tell him no again.

I had less than an hour to get dressed and on the road. I knew the drive into Omaha would take at least thirty minutes, so that meant I had to get moving. I scribbled a quick note for Callum and Moose, telling them I'd be back and not to worry. They'd be able to get into the house without me there. I threw on a pair of jeans and a sweater, grabbed my coat, and ran out of the door. Fall temperatures in Nebraska could change quickly and I couldn't handle the cold well. Another change I'd learned to accommodate. I ran to the large garage and my favorite car. Sliding into the seat, I relaxed back, my eyes closing as I leaned against the head rest. I could hear Angus again, chuckling when he saw me in this car. "Two Hellcats for the price of one," he'd said. "Just don't kill yourself driving too fast on these back roads."

I drove calmly down the gravel road away from my house, but once I hit pavement, I let myself enjoy the feel of the road flying underneath me. I sang along with the radio as loud as I could, since there was no one to hear me.

Arriving at the coffee shop the detective had wanted us to meet at, I maneuvered my way into the only parking space open. That left me a short walk over the old bricks of the original street. I loved the historic part of this city, but those damn things could be ankle killers.

Detective Bishop was seated at a table in the back, away from the windows. He must have sensed that I didn't want to be recognized. I tried to appreciate his consideration but couldn't shake off the foreboding I felt. I ordered some hot tea at the counter and the detective joined me, ordering himself a fancy coffee and something to snack on. I took my drink to the table he'd claimed and sat down, my back solidly against the wall, limiting the ways I might be surprised.

When he joined me at the table, he tried to make conversation. He worked his way through the small talk checklist, finally apologizing for our meeting earlier in the day. He needed to get the real story and the best way to do that was to catch me off guard. Surely I could understand that.

I held up my hands for him to stop. "Listen. I'm almost done with my tea and I don't like small talk. So, I'm going to the counter there to refresh my drink and when I come back, you're going to tell me what was so damned important that you made me come meet you here. If I don't have the answer by the time I'm done drinking my tea, I'm leaving, and you will not contact me again." I didn't let him say anything, just got up and did exactly what I said I would. By the time I was ready to sit back down, he'd chewed his way through the fruit bar he'd purchased and was nervously jiggling his leg.

As I sat down, he glanced up at me from the table, then back down. "I'm sorry. This is harder to do than I thought it would be. But it's just too important not to tell you."

He pulled a couple pictures from his jacket and laid them face down on the table in front of me but didn't remove his hand. I didn't want to see any more pictures of me at the club or anywhere else for that matter, so I didn't reach for them.

"I know this will be hard for you, but I think it's important you know what's happened since that night in Angel Falls," he said keeping his voice low.

I sucked in a shocked breath as he turned them over. In each picture, a woman was laid out on the ground. One was wearing the same devil costume I'd used at the club, a curly blonde wig askew. The other was wearing a costume that looked very much like the angel costume I'd worn once while I waited for the murderer to show. I remembered that I'd worn a bright color of lipstick, probably borrowed from one of the dancers that night. The woman in front of me had the same color on her lips, but it had been smudged, as if someone had kissed her roughly. Both women had been strangled, telling bruises left behind on their throats. I closed my eyes, overwhelmed by the sensation of strong hands wrapped around my neck and the agony as I struggled to breathe.

"Are you all right, Delaney?" Detective Bishop's voice was soft.

I shook off the lingering panic I felt, refusing to give in to the memory. "Why are you showing me these?"

"Because you need to know. Looking at these pictures, all I can see is their resemblance to you. I think whoever did this, he was working with the guy you killed. Maybe he was there at the club, scoping things out. He saw you and when you stopped his partner, he decided that you needed to go. But you left town, and now, he's working his way to you. Killing women who look like you in the process."

I forced myself to look at the pictures again. Closely. "But, they don't look like me." And they really didn't. They were wearing the same clothes, the same hair and makeup maybe, but if you were able to look past those things, you could see we weren't matches. Both of them were obviously taller and more slender than I could ever hope to be.

"Close enough to be your stand-in for this guy. And when these girls went missing, they weren't dressed like this. He put them in these costumes, made them look like you."

I wanted to keep my voice low, but could feel fear building inside me, making it hard to breathe. I tried to be calm, but my words trembled as I spoke. "I haven't seen anything about this. I have online alerts set up to notify me if anything like the other deaths were reported. Nothing has come through."

"It's been kept out of the media for now. But if this keeps happening, it'll be everywhere soon. And the part you played in this won't stay hidden long."

I was responsible for this, that's what he was saying. I tried to sip my drink and give my heart time to slow down to its regular pace, but I couldn't. I pushed away from the table and dashed down the dimly lit hallway to the women's restroom. Inside, alone, I ran cold water in the sink, using it to wash away the tears that had started to fall. Despite what I'd tried to do, despite wanting to keep other women from being hurt, I was the reason two more had died. I remembered what it had felt like to have those hands around my throat, to be desperate and gasping for air. The pain of it blossomed fiercely in my chest even as I fought to regain my control.

When I could look in the mirror again, I was shocked at how white my face was. My eyes were wide, the shock still evident, and my lips stood out, a slash of bright red against my skin. I didn't want any of this to be true. But that didn't change the fact this had happened. Would likely happen again. I needed information to catch this guy and end whatever game he thought he was playing.

Knowing I had to face the harsh facts, I whispered to myself. "You have to go back out there. Hiding won't do any good now." I bit my lip, straightened my shoulders, and stepped out into the hallway.

Strong hands grabbed me, pushing me up against a wall. I felt like everything slowed down, moving forward in minute increments. I dazedly recognized Detective Bishop, beautiful eyes fierce as he looked down at me. He glanced over his shoulder, toward the seating area, his fingers just grazing the skin over my collarbone. The small accidental touch shocked me, and it felt so good. I gasped pulling the detective's attention back to me, the dark centers of his eyes eating up the bright blue surrounding them. He leaned in, his tongue wetting his lips, but I could feel restraint thrumming in him. Holding him back. I heard the whisper leave my mouth before the thought had fully formed in my mind. One word. "Yes."

A triumphant smile flared on his face before his lips crashed down on mine, demanding. My mouth opened in surprise, letting his tongue in. I couldn't move, and the kiss slowed down, an exploration. When I didn't resist, his hands moved into my hair, tangling his fingers in the curls. I leaned into that touch. Heat pulsed through me and desire rose up fiercely, my stomach fluttering. I wanted more, so much more. Suddenly I was kissing him back, tasting him the way he had tasted me. He moaned softly, and his hands moved from my hair to cup my face and then down to my arms, holding me firmly between him and the wall.

As he broke away to take a shaky breath, sense began to

force its way back into my brain, reminding me I shouldn't be doing this. I pushed at his arms, trying to break the connection. I was in danger of falling, losing myself in how wonderful it felt to be held. To be desired. But I couldn't let it happen. I had to stop this. I ground the heel of my shoe into the top of Torren's foot. He flinched away, and I was able to step out of his embrace, putting some much-needed distance between us.

His gaze was unfocused, the blue of his eyes replaced by a deep darkness. A soft grin spread across his face as he said, "You taste good. Sweet with a little spice. Hot." He closed his eyes, swaying like he was drunk, and when he opened them again, he said, "So good." Need layered those simple words and he took a step toward me, like he wanted to taste me again.

I held my hands up, backing away from him, down the hall to where the tables were. I needed to maintain a healthy amount of space between us. "We shouldn't have done that," I said, trying to keep my voice calm.

"I'm sorry. I was just waiting out here to make sure you were okay." He pleaded with me, each step he took bringing him closer to me. His voice was almost a purr, silky against my ears and I fought to resist its pull. My body desperately wanted me to close the gap between us, to let him kiss me again and see if it felt as good a third time. And a fourth. And on and on.

"No Torren. Please. We can't."

He kept talking, the rhythm of his voice pulling me in. "When you left the table, I saw this guy. I think he was looking for you. When you came out..." he stopped, confused. Shaking his head, clearing it, he continued. "I'm not sure why I did that. But it felt good. Perfect."

The panic in me rose to the top when I felt heat between us snap into being again as he reached for me. I slipped away from him. "You don't understand what just happened."

"I understand exactly what we did. I kissed you. We liked it." He kept coming toward me, daring me to deny it.

"That's not what I meant. You can't just kiss me. This is a problem." I knew I was babbling, fear making me ramble. "I have to go."

He reached out again. "Stay, please. Or I'll come with you. If that man I saw is following you, I can't let you go alone."

I dodged his grasping hand. "No. You need to go back to wherever it is you're staying. Take a very cold shower, get some sleep. Do anything but think about what happened here."

"But, Delaney," he started. I cut him off with a wave of my hand and a quick shake of my head.

"Go. Now!" I turned and ran through the cafe, past the chairs and the customers ordering. Out in the cold air, I realized I'd left my coat behind. But I wasn't going back, not with Torren still there, high on what we'd done. I'd used my magic around him from the first time we met, and he'd followed me home. Things had just gone from bad to worse. We needed to stay away from each other.

This was yet another problem for me to fix. Angus was going to be so completely pissed.

Chapter Fourteen

My hands were shaking when I made it to my car, the cold chill of panic taking me over. My heart hammered in my head and I kept hearing Torren's voice, the soft way he said my name. I jerked the transmission into reverse and slammed my foot down on the gas, ignoring the high whine of the engine at my rough treatment. Horns sounded behind me, but I didn't spare a look back. I had to get out of there.

I spotted Torren, following the path I'd taken to my parking space as if he was a born tracker. My feet jammed down hard on the clutch and brake, the tires protesting even as I shifted violently into first gear. The tires spun as I dumped the clutch and mashed the gas again. The back end slid to the right before it hooked up and my Hellcat jumped forward, racing toward my escape.

I didn't look back until I was surrounded by empty countryside. No cars were visible in my rearview, and I tried to slow my breathing. Tears had fallen as I drove, leaving salty tracks down my face as they dried. I couldn't go home like this. I saw the turn off to an old gravel road up ahead and took it, following it away from the highway until it bent around the curve of a hill and I was hidden from view by the slope and a stand of trees. I pulled off to the side and stopped, resting my head on the wheel. Silent sobs shook me, and I gave in, the memories of the last time I'd been kissed sweeping over and pulling me under, back into that night two years ago. Angus had come to me, after my prom had erupted into mayhem at the sudden emergence of my magic. He'd given me a choice.

"All of it? All that happened because of you?" I faced him, tears blurring my vision. I didn't want to believe what he'd just told me, but gut deep, I knew every word had been true. The screams from the gym still echoed in my ears.

"No Delaney. It happened because of you." He gave me a sad smile. "The sins of the father and all that."

The room swam as I fought to catch a breath. My mother. My friends. My future. Everything I thought my life would be was slipping away and there was nothing I could do.

"You have to make a choice." This time his voice was softer. "Stay or go. You have to decide."

I forced myself to swallow against the bile in my throat. "That's not a choice, Dad. But you already knew that."

He didn't say anything, but he didn't look away. No matter what, he would be my witness.

"Go. It's the right thing to do." As I choked the words out, an agonized scream rose up from the hall right outside the room I'd hidden in, as if somehow my answer had penetrated the walls. I recognized the voice that called my name, pleading with me not to leave as a heavy fist battered the door I'd locked behind me. My heart twisted in my chest, a pain I almost welcomed. But the decision was made. I nodded at my father, more strength in my answer this time. "I have to go."

"That's my girl."

He came to stand behind me, strong arms wrapping around and pulling me close, snuggling me up against his heart. The scent of brimstone stung my nose even as it comforted me. Then he took one step back and we fell, together, into Hell.

I tore myself free of the memory. Darkness had settled in outside my window, the stars bright in the cloudless sky, and silence wrapped itself around me, only my ragged breathing breaking the quiet. I couldn't sit here all night. Cal and Moose would be waiting for me, wondering where I was. I started the engine, and let the car roll forward. Gravel crunched as I angled the tires back onto the road, leaving my moment of weakness behind.

WHEN I GOT HOME, lights were blazing out onto the bare ground, making me aware of how late it was. I parked and locked the garage, then walked methodically to the house, stepping around the holes I knew from painful experience were there. I needed to have them filled in but hadn't gotten around to it.

Opening the front door, the conversation I'd interrupted came to an immediate halt. In my dining room, Callum was seated at the table with my father and a tall man with shaggy hair and a gray beard. I was so happy to see him there I couldn't stop the surprised laugh that fell out of me.

"Hi, Uncle Newt," I said, trying not to sound desperate as I gave him a hug.

"Hey Laney Girl," he answered, squeezing me hard in return. When I released him, he looked me directly in the eyes and gestured to an empty chair. "Seems like we need to have a talk."

I sat down and realized that I'd been sandwiched between Angus and Newton. Callum was tense, his jaw tight. Moose lay on the floor next to my father, his allegiance clear. Newt patted me on the back, making me feel like a little kid again.

"So, what do you want to talk about?" I asked, even though I already knew.

"First off, Callum's told us what happened with the detective," Newt said. "He tracked you down using the money. Which was smart." I started to protest but he kept talking. "Now, nobody would've ever guessed he'd do that. No one had any real reason to dig that deep. You did everything you could to set things up so you'd be forgotten about. Hard to trace. But you couldn't have expected this. Nobody here faults you for this little mistake." He looked at my father, who remained stony silent, then said again, "Nobody faults you for any of this. And you had good intentions when you thought to use the account for the shelter."

Then my father spoke, his voice humorless. "You know what they say about good intentions. Paving the road to Hell and all."

I kept my eyes focused on the tabletop, following the wood grain as it flowed from one pattern to another.

"But we have to decide what to do about him, now that he's found you," Newt said, continuing to address the problem. "Callum thinks he's planning to stick around and dig into your background some more. That would be bad. For him and for you."

Truth time. I covered my face and counted to ten, listening to the rhythm of my heart, a staccato pounding inside my head. Newt had taught me this during our early training sessions, when my flares of emotion had gotten me in trouble. Focusing on the steady beat inside my head forced the feelings to calm. Opening my eyes, I looked at each of the men around me. "It's worse than you think." I took a breath, then let the words tumble out. "He kissed me tonight. At the coffee shop. He said he wanted to meet with me, because there were two more dead women, and then he thought some guy was looking for me, so he tried to hide me. But then he kissed me."

My father's eyes flashed red with anger and I flinched when Callum's hand smacked the table. Newt had frozen in place. Even Moose had lifted his head up, his serious eyes trained on me. They were all waiting for me to finish.

"He didn't want me to leave after that. But I told him to go back to his hotel and sleep this off. Then I ran."

All of us looked at Angus, who had been watching me intently during this exchange. He cleared his throat. "Did you feel anything at all when he kissed you? Anything unusual?"

I nodded. "Electric, like a shock. Not when he first grabbed me. But when his fingers brushed over my skin, it happened. Then he kissed me."

Angus closed his eyes for a moment. "I was afraid this would happen. You've been alone so long. I hoped that having Callum and the Hound out here would ease things for you. When you were at the club those weeks, you didn't feed at all." It wasn't a question, it was a statement; he already knew how hard I'd worked to survive without pulling from the energy of people around me.

I shook my head. "Newt taught me how to shield myself from others, so I wouldn't be taking from people without meaning to. When Torren grabbed me, I was so surprised I must have let my guard down without realizing it."

"It's Torren now, not Detective?" asked Callum, his voice rough.

I hadn't caught the slip myself and blushed.

Newt let out a long breath. "You're right. This is a lot worse. We have to finish it."

"No. You can't hurt him. He didn't know what he was doing." I couldn't let Torren's life be ruined because of me. "Please. We have to help him."

Angus and Newt stared at each other, no doubt sharing thoughts between themselves. After minutes of silence, Newt stood up from the table and walked out of the room, kissing me quickly on the cheek as he walked by. His leaving so immediately without a word of goodbye frightened me. This had to be bad.

My father laid his hand over mine, trying to comfort me. When I could meet his gaze, he said, "Delaney, I'm afraid you've Bound him, whether you meant to or not. Newton is going to check in on him, see if there's anything that can be done to reverse this. But you must stop acting like your magic is a poison. It's part of who you are, a power you can use wisely if you choose to. It doesn't have to be a bad thing."

"How can you say that? You know what this did to Mom. That's the reason you left, why we had to watch your plane crash and go to that damn funeral. Why we have to endure it over and over again, every year." Angus winced at my words, but I pressed on. "Mom lost everything she loved because of this."

My father was motionless as my words faded out, pain in his eyes. I swallowed, regret blocking my throat. Angus refused to let me look away, raising his hand up to my chin, holding me gently in place. "I could never forgive myself for your mother's illness. That's why I left the way I did. Had any of us known that my choosing to stay with the two of you instead of continuing to tour regularly would have hurt her like that, I'd have left immediately. No one knew you'd inherit my abilities the way you have." I opened my mouth to interrupt but he held up a hand to stop me. "Or that they would manifest the way they did. How they would affect people. We dealt with that."

"We agreed we'd never talk about that again." I kept my voice low, the words wooden, not allowing any emotion to show.

"You asked me not to. I feel it has some bearing on the situation you're in now." This was his patented dad voice, forced calm overlaying the true emotion running underneath. "If I could have prevented what happened to your mother, I would have. If I could have kept this gift from you, I would have done that too. I hate that it's caused you pain."

I knew all of this, knew how much my father had loved his family, even my unborn brother that never lived to join us. Angus had realized too late the effect he was having on my mother's pregnancy and, despite calling in everyone possible to assist, there had been no way to save the baby. My father's need for energy, normally satisfied by the adoring crowds at his concerts, had meant he was unwittingly siphoning energy from my mother and brother once he chose to remain at home. He'd planned out his exit in perfect detail, a death worthy of any true rock star, the plane crashing right after takeoff with him and all members of The Law on board. It was splashed across every newspaper, magazine cover, and television screen for countless weeks. The last public photos of my mother and me had been taken at his funeral. Mom had said goodbye to the home we'd shared as a growing family, moved me to her family's ranch, and turned down all requests for interviews. She was a grieving widow and wanted to be left alone.

With Angus gone, my mother's strength had gradually returned, and she was healthier. Healthy and alone, missing the man she loved. And she was without me too—once we'd realized that my body had started to thrive on the energy of others, I refused to see her again. I was never going to put her at risk.

"You should have considered my offer to set you up with a band, Delaney. You love to sing. Performing would have allowed you to meet your needs and not connected you too deeply with any one person. Neglecting that has led us to this."

I shook my head. I sang in public one time. One time only. I'd been standing on the edges of the dance floor, swaying with the music and singing the lyrics quietly. I'd gotten lost in the sound and hadn't realized I was drawing a crowd. I remembered how the energy had felt, the sweet taste as I'd pulled it into myself without understanding what

I was doing. When the music finally trailed off, a ragged riff that ended with silence other than my voice, I opened my eyes, surprised at the number of people that surrounded me. One of them reached out to touch me and I stepped back, bumping into someone else. There was pushing and shoving, and then people were tugging at me from all directions. I screamed, the sound echoing, shrill and hurt, off the high ceiling. Some people cowered at the sound while a few fled. And one of them, Brett, began tearing the room apart as he tried to reach me. He was my prom date. He'd kissed me at the end of our last dance, right before he'd gone to get us drinks. My first kiss. Not exactly a romantic memory I liked to reminisce about. He'd hurt people that night. I could still hear him begging me not to leave, screaming that I was his as police who'd come to the scene took him away in handcuffs. That was the night Angus had come, had given me a choice. Stay where I was or join him Below. I learned a lot in my time away. And my decision to stop the demon who was hunting down women had been my first experience at attempting to manage regular contact with people since I'd returned.

Thinking back, I wondered about Brett. My one and only date. He'd been a good guy. Until it all fell apart. I couldn't help but wonder where he was now.

"Dad, have you had anyone check on Brett? To see if he started to improve after I left, I mean?"

My father nodded quickly. "I promised you I would.

Newt's been keeping an eye on him. When you first left, Brett deteriorated very quickly. He was undergoing treatment, living with his parents. He was making progress."

"There have been more women murdered. That's what Torren, I mean, Detective Bishop, wanted me to know."

"And why did he feel it was important you be given this information specifically?"

I sighed. Best to just be honest. "He showed me pictures of them. They were both dressed like me. Like I'd been at the club. Even the same hair. And they were strangled." I shivered remembering the marks on their throats. Those bruises were a frightening reminder of how close I'd come to losing that fight.

My father's green eyes narrowed, considering the implications of this. "So, he was there, saw you that night."

"It's worse than that. I think he saw me other nights, as well. They were wearing two different costumes, two different wigs." At my father's questioning look, I said, "An angel and a devil."

Cal whistled low, then said, "So, he not only saw you, he studied you. Enough to remember how you styled each costume, the wigs you used. Did you notice anyone paying more attention to you than normal?"

I shook my head. "Not really. There were always guys making comments or trying to get a girl's attention, but nothing out of the ordinary. And I wasn't a dancer—all I did was get drinks and make sure no one skipped out on their tab."

Callum laughed softly and when I looked at him with anger, he held his hands up in defense. "Laney, don't take this the wrong way, but you don't realize how hard it is not to notice you. Whether you were dancing or not wouldn't have mattered. People see you."

Chapter Fifteen

EXHAUSTION TOOK ME as soon as I slid beneath my sheets and I welcomed the sleep. I was so very tired, every bit of me worn through by all that had happened. But instead of rest, I found myself falling into a dusty dream world, everything black and white, except for splashes of crimson that appeared from time to time. The bright spots were clearly spatters of blood on the pavement or grass, bushes, and even the walls of buildings. I walked deserted streets and saw abandoned homes, doors standing wide open, possessions spilled out into yards and driveways. Silence screamed at me.

It felt like I stumbled through this landscape for hours, alone and unsure. Fear wormed its way through me, until it seemed like there were eyes watching from every shadow, every corner. And when my legs were about to give way, the muscles fatigued and aching, I began to hear a clear voice ringing through the starless night. One voice singing out, calling for people to come and be safe, to join with others in the truth that promised salvation. I followed, discovering others ahead of me and struggled forward faster to walk with them, until the trickle of bodies became a crowd gathered at the base of a hill, worshiping the one who stood upon it.

As the swell of people increased, the voice grew louder, gaining power and sway over any who stood below. New voices rose up, carrying the call to surrender and have faith. We would each be lifted up, delivered from the devastation threatening to overwhelm us. And still, above it all, the siren song continued, gaining power from those gathered near, until the press of bodies was so heavy that it was difficult to move, and it felt like I would be crushed. The murmurs and cries of the crowd were angry and pained now, demanding justice and leadership, promising service and unending allegiance. An army seething, waiting for release.

The frantic voices rose in pitch and the moon began to move from behind the clouds, a spotlight slowly shifting into place. As the pleas of everyone gathered peaked, the clear light landed full on the figure that had first sent out the call to come. Fevered cries erupted, and I swore I could hear weeping around me. On that mound, the recognizable face of my father was clear to all, the miracle of his presence securing the loyalty of the horde now swearing to serve him. Shadows swirled behind him, constant movement that framed him perfectly. Screams of exaltation swelled and I tried to push against the crush that held me in place, tried to reach the stage he stood upon and stop this, recognizing madness in his eyes. But I was pushed to the ground by his ardent followers and the weight of their bodies held me down until I couldn't fight back or even gather breath to cry out for help.

My father's voice rose to a crescendo and the crowd came to a halt, their weight still poised above me. A harsh note rang out and the weight bearing me into the ground was released, bodies flung off me until there was a small clearing in which I could struggle upright. I panted, dragging in air, doubled over and mentally checking for wounds or broken bones.

"Hear me now!" Angus cried out, his voice so strong it overwhelmed the crowd. "This is my child, who has made me very proud." I looked up to find him pointing down at me, the eyes of everyone focused where he directed. "She will lead with me, my right hand, and together we will bring about the promised victory!"

Crazed cheers and maddened calls for battle broke out as the people parted before me. I made my way to the hill where my father happily surveyed his followers. Demons were darting behind him, the shadows I'd seen as I approached. I climbed to the top, my feet slipping in the loose dirt, my nails breaking as I tried to steady myself and move forward.

Finally reaching the top, the demons made way for me as

I passed them. I searched the faces I could see, hoping for someone familiar that would help me reason with my father and break the spell he had cast, but there was no one I recognized. When I made it to the front, Angus turned to me, a strange smile on his face as he grabbed my arm and pulled me to him. He gestured to the wasteland around us and the people milling about below. Fires flared up, the scene reminding of an ancient battlefield encampment.

"See Delaney, I have given you the world. Now all we have to do is go out and take what is ours."

I shook my head in disbelief. My mouth was dry, but I forced out the words. "This isn't you, Angus. You wouldn't do this."

His eyes bore into me, the flames below reflected in his pupils. "But I would. For you, I would do anything."

I woke drenched in sweat with tears still wet on my cheeks. An urgent awareness filled me, a warning that I had seen a very possible future, one where my father led an army of followers in the wake of some devastating event. There had been promises in the songs he'd used to draw people to him, the power of his voice luring people to his cause. Promises they would be protected, part of a better world to come. One where he would rule. This couldn't be allowed to happen. I needed help and I knew exactly where I had to go.

Chapter Sixteen

Driving the dusty roads from my home into town was usually relaxing, the surrounding trees and wild growing things a shifting patchwork of colors that eased the mind. Today, though, my mind was racing, and the trip didn't work its usual magic on me. The town of Hazelwood, Nebraska, was several miles away from my home and there were plenty of twists and roller coaster hills that had your stomach butterflying inside if you rode them too fast. I tried to let go and enjoy them the way I normally would, but I couldn't. Maybe it was the lingering effects of the dream. Or the fact that I had two passengers riding beside me in what was usually an empty car. I just couldn't bring myself to roll the windows down for a breath of the cool fall weather or sing my heart out with the car radio. I felt restrained and claustrophobic.

I tried to explain Hazelwood to Callum and Moose. It

was a different place, warm and filled with its own magic. I rarely went into town, but over the past few years, the people of Hazelwood had become accustomed to seeing me. Alone. My arrival with two new shadows would trigger a flood of interest through a town of people who knew everyone who came and went. They'd want to know if these guests were going to stay. I had no answer for that question myself.

When I pulled onto the paved highway from the county road that connected my land to the town, I floored the accelerator, not hiding how much I wanted to get this trip over and done with. Some things had to be done and I couldn't dodge them any longer. We flew into the town, and I slowed only as we drew near the business area. The old stones of these streets could be hard on the car and I babied it. My destination was in the heart of the old downtown. The one place where everyone in Hazelwood came when a need arose.

"Remind me again why we had to come here?" Callum asked.

I sighed. "Miss Tilly. She knows everything that goes on in or around Hazelwood. She used to own the land I live on and she's still tied to it. If something's coming this way, she'll know." I had no doubt about that, but the question really was whether Miss Tilly would share her knowledge with me.

"And you don't want me coming in with you? Are you sure you'll be safe?"

"She isn't going to hurt me. And bringing you in without her invitation would be rude. Miss Tilly doesn't tolerate rudeness. Anyone in town will tell you that."

"Well, we can't just sit in the car while you talk to this woman, you know."

"You don't have to. You can get out, walk around. Go window shopping, buy a snack at the diner. The pie there is the very best, by the way." I stopped wanting to make sure I impressed upon him how very important my next words were. "Just don't follow me in there. When I'm done, I'll come right back to the car. If you're not there, someone will tell me where you are."

"Really? You think they'll watch us that closely."

I snorted, slowing as we turned right onto Adair Street. "I know it. Without a doubt."

He didn't question me further, just sat quietly until I parked along the curb near Miss Tilly's and started to take my seat belt off. He laid a hand on my arm and asked with only a raised eyebrow if I was sure. I nodded to him, said goodbye to Moose with a gentle rub of his ears, and stepped out on the red cobbles of the street. They were uneven but familiar, with a low energy thrumming through them.

Hazelwood was small but prosperous, known for keeping its historic charms intact and offering products that many people from the larger surrounding towns and cities appreciated. Organic honey, fresh milk and butter, bread and pies baked daily brought people in. The orchard we'd passed on the way into town had the most delicious peaches you could find. There was a quilter who specialized in personalizing traditional patterns, melding the old with the new. The hardware store had everything, aisles stretching impossibly far back, and the owner knew where each little bit and part would be.

Even the beautiful old Victorian home at the end of the block was a popular bed and breakfast, owned by a woman named Donna Kay, whose family had lived here forever. She also ran the town's only salon, which was in the back of the house, and knew all the gossip. People told her everything and she had a definite knack for figuring things out, whether you wanted her to or not. She'd invited me in for a cut and style shortly after I'd moved to the area. When I declined, she'd kindly whispered that she had figured out who my father was but promised not to say anything to anyone. Except maybe to Miss Tilly, of course. I'd laughed at that. Miss Tilly knew what I was as soon as we met to finalize the property purchase. And she hadn't cared. She'd just looked at me, nodded, and said, "Yes, you're the right one for this place." Things might be changing around Hazelwood, but somehow, the traditions held on. Strong and true.

Miss Tilly's little shop was in the center, every other business grouped around it and spreading out in rings from there. The only identifier on the old, beautifully worn red building was lettering on the leaded glass of the large front window, spelling out THE HEDGEROW in carefully swirling letters. Pushing open the front door, I could pick up the soft sweet scent of something candied mixed with citrus and cinnamon riding the comfortably cool air. Bins ran along the walls, glass jars showcasing the different herbs and teas available, mixtures to aid in diet or to relieve stress. There was even one to promote lactation for new mothers. Almond and lavender soaps, handmade by Miss Tilly's granddaughter, were featured in a display on the right, their scents soothing and inviting.

Behind the glass case, standing proudly in the soft light, was a wisp of a woman, smaller than me even. But no one who ever got a glimpse of her proud face and silver hair thought she was weak. She radiated strength. The look in the sharp eyes behind her delicate glasses told me she'd been expecting me. And I was late.

"So, the Girl has finally arrived. And about time. I've been waiting." Her voice was soft, but it carried in the quiet store. "She has strange visitors and badness is sneaking toward us all. Still she takes so long to come talk with me. Why?"

I stepped closer to the glass case but didn't touch it. This was her domain and until she invited me further, I would wait and answer her questions. Because, if I was honest with her, she might agree to answer mine.

"I thought I could handle things on my own, Miss Tilly. I was trying to. But there are too many things I don't understand. I had a dream last night, one that woke me up I was so afraid. That's when I realized I needed to come to you."

She nodded. "You've always worked too hard to hold the world away from you. Ever since you first came here, we all felt how you pushed people away. Never trusting that some were strong enough to lift you up."

Miss Tilly turned away from me without waiting for a response, moving to the tea set she had waiting in the corner of the shop. Two overstuffed, antique chairs framed the little area near a sunlit window perfectly and they gleamed as if they were brand new. She gestured me forward as she sat and began to pour into the two cups she'd put out.

"Sit down Girl. No one else is coming. It is your time and we have much to discuss before you have to go."

I followed her instructions, sinking down onto the chair and relaxing back into its softness. Miss Tilly's was one of the safest places I had ever been in. Nothing would dare invade her space. I sipped the tea she handed me and waited. Patience was important in this room, a hard lesson I'd learned in the short time I'd lived here.

She sipped and swallowed warm, flavorful apple tea, spiced with cinnamon and something stronger I suspected, watching me silently until she set her tea cup down and leaned back, her posture matching mine in apparent relaxation. Still, I kept my mouth shut. Hard lessons but I'm a quick learner when I need to be.

Finally, she nodded and whispered to me. "The battle you've been fighting is wearing you down Girl. You've tried to do too much alone and you're tired. Pieces of you are frayed and starting to wear." She gestured at me, waving her thin hands from my windblown hair down to the tennis shoes I'd slipped on. I knew she wasn't really referring to my exterior but seeing deeper. "It is time to accept the help that is given you. Strength that you need, that will help you to heal. It is time." She returned to her tea, sipping it again until she'd drained the cup and then filled it again.

I held my own warm cup in my hands, feeling the gold filigree bite into my skin just a bit. I waited, but she didn't say anything else. This was a sign it was my turn.

"You're right, Miss Tilly. I thought I could do this all myself, but everything I've seen proves I'm wrong. There's a bigger problem circling, and I haven't been able to figure it out. It's almost as if every time my mind is about to unravel things, it becomes foggy again and I lose the thread. I'm trying to protect everyone, and I can't even figure out what the threat is that has me so worried."

She smiled sadly, pouring more tea into the cup I'd unconsciously emptied. "It is the badness. You are a smart one, Girl, and it knows this. It sends things to trick you and frighten, to make you question yourself and steal your strength. You must work your way back through this. The biggest trick will come from your past. A past you are ashamed of."

My hand froze on the way to my mouth, for just a moment. I tried to pass it off as nothing by taking a drink, but I knew she'd noticed. She leaned forward, her hands now gripping mine as I set the cup down, afraid of the shaking that had started in my fingers. I didn't want to damage the heirloom china I was sure had been passed down to her. Her steel voice rang out, her hold on my hands unbreakable. "Shame is lies, Girl. Remember, for every saint in the world, there is a past they run from. For every sinner, there is a future they can run toward." She dropped my hands then, patting them as they rested on the small tabletop. "I know you Girl. I see you as I always have. You live your life out there, trying to do no harm. Like all of us here. But when harm comes looking, then you must do what needs to be done. Without fear. Only strength."

Her gentle brown eyes never left mine, and I held my breath, wanting to know exactly what this harm would be. When her eyes started to fill with tears, she looked down, using a fabric napkin from the table to dab the water away, I forced myself to breathe again. "There are some things you will need. I have them ready for you." She stood up and walked back to the shelves behind her display case, opening a drawer and pulling out a package already wrapped up in brown paper. "It is $25.50. Cash only please."

I felt weak, the shakes working their way through me before I could safely stand. I pulled thirty dollars out of my purse, walked over to Miss Tilly and handed it over to her.

She put it in the register and nodded to me. No change. I hadn't really expected any. It was her way. I quietly thanked her and turned to go. As I reached the door and was about to pull it open to step back onto the street, I heard her say, "Next time, Girl. Bring your boys. They will need to meet me. As will the Hound." I nodded back at her and continued out the door. The invitation had been given and I would make sure to do as I was told. As the door swung shut, I heard her say one final thing. "Call your mother, Girl. She needs to hear your voice."

CHAPTER SEVENTEEN

WALKING BACK toward my car, I recognized one of the men walking on the other side of Adair Street. I raised my hand in a brief wave, which he returned before pointing ahead of me to where I knew the diner sat on the opposite corner. The corner of his mouth quirked up for a moment, as if he wasn't quite able to hide a smile and then he walked on, leaving me standing alone on a street that I realized was oddly empty for this time of day.

I hurried across the street, my attention focused on the brightly painted door of the town's most well-known restaurant. Everyone in the state had heard of Anita's, the diner with the bright green door, where the food was homemade and the owner unafraid to offer her loud advice about exactly what might be bothering you in life. Hamburger buns fresh out of the oven, cinnamon rolls as big as the plate with frosting dripping down off the sides and freshly ground coffee brewing all day long. It was a welcoming place for people, the homey scents and laughter building a need to come back. Working its own magic.

I shoved open the door without stopping, hearing the chimes above ring out as I stepped in. Everyone inside turned to look at me. There were far too many people crowded into a small space. Every stool at the counter was full, every table and booth taken. Some customers were even leaning against the wall where I came in. Anita, the owner herself, was standing at a booth in the back of the diner, hands on her broad hips, a sunflower apron around her waist. Her hair was pulled up into a tight bun, threads of gray running through the black in even lines. Not even her hair would defy her by daring to attempt an escape.

Seeing me, she gestured quickly, narrowed eyes telling me to hurry it up. I lengthened my stride as much as I could, but it felt like I walked past staring eyes and whispers forever before I made it to her side. As I stepped up beside Anita, Callum came into view, his head resting back against the booth, a content look on his face and his hands resting on his belly. Across from him, seated on the booth, with his head resting on the table edge, was Moose in his cute terrier form. His eyes were closed and as I stood there, a satisfied sigh escaped him. There were the remnants of what looked like apple pie strewn across the tabletop.

"Oh Anita," I gasped out, trying very hard not to laugh. "I'm so sorry. Did they eat a whole pie?"

"Two. Two whole pies!" she barked out. "And how that dog was able to sneak in here, I'd like to know. Everybody swears it was just this one, sitting here ordering pie, until I walk out to help some other customers and find this mutt with his head on my table."

Hearing himself called a mutt, Moose opened one eye to look at the angry woman next to me, before closing it and sighing again. He was clearly so happy and full of deliciousness that he couldn't even be offended. When I'd mentioned that Anita's pies were good, I'd never dreamed this would be the situation I'd find.

Cal chose that second to intervene, stretching his arms up over his head like he was just waking up. "Ma'am, let me just tell you how amazing that pie is. Delaney told me that you made the best pies she'd ever tasted, but I couldn't imagine the exquisite delight waiting behind your green door. Truly, delicious. And the homemade ice cream I had to go with it was the perfect complement." Then he grabbed Anita's hand and shook it. "I apologize for my companion, but knowing his love of apples, I couldn't keep this from him."

Anita was frozen, her eyes taking in Cal's sincere expression, and what I'm sure she found to be a very handsome face. I held my breath and it sounded like everyone behind me did as well. Finally, she slid her hand out of his, turning to me and whispering in a flustered tone, "Next time, they can take it outside if the dog wants to eat pie." She dashed back into the kitchen, giggles starting up among the customers that had gathered to see the fireworks.

Cal watched me, laughter dancing across his face, and I grinned at him. "I leave you alone for a few minutes and you manage to find a way to piss off the best cook in this entire town. She probably wants to ban me from this place."

"Guess it's a good thing I'm so charming then," he threw back at me.

"Yeah. Must be all those romance novels you've been reading."

He flashed a smile at me. "Newton told me studying those would help me acclimate to this world faster. That I would understand people better and learn how to talk with them."

I snorted. "People? Or women?" I set cash on top of the bill Anita had left for the pie. No one would steal it. Not in Hazelwood.

"Now Delaney," he chided me, sliding his long legs out of the booth and following as I led the way out of the diner and to my car, "women are people too, you know."

I shook my head, knowing that anything I could possibly say would only encourage him. Instead, we headed for home, the radio blasting some Angus Murphy and The Law. We couldn't help but laugh as Moose tried to howl along at the chorus. Terribly.

Chapter Eighteen

WHEN WE GOT HOME, Cal and Moose busied themselves with patrolling the property and making sure the wards they'd set earlier were holding. At Cal's suggestion, we'd added additional protection wards along the fence line and around the garage. They weren't as strong as the ones directly around the house, but they offered us some additional security. They had a lot of ground to cover, but the night was cool and pleasant. I think they both needed time to stretch their legs and work together on this. I went inside alone, taking advantage of the quiet to call my mother.

As the phone rang on the other end, I wondered about the things Miss Tilly had said. She took the security of Hazelwood seriously and if she was worried about evil coming this way, then it promised to be bad. I was biting my lip when I heard the click as the call was picked up.

"Hello?" came my mother's voice on the line.

I swallowed against a sudden lump in my throat. Careful to keep my magic locked away, I said, "Hey Mom. How are you?"

"Delaney, oh wow, I've been hoping to hear from you. Don't worry about me. How are you?"

"I'm fine. Keeping up with everything as best I can."

"You're doing a great job with the foundation. Things are so much more organized with you handling stuff." I heard a smile in her voice when she said that. She'd never enjoyed being the one in charge of everything, but she'd done it. This was a way to make things better for others and she loved to volunteer her time at events but managing the day-to-day work had never been her dream.

"How are the horses?" I asked.

"Oh, Junior is fine. He nicked himself on the leg the other day and it keeps trying to get infected, so we've been watching it. But other than that, he's his same sassy self. Bella still loves bossing everyone around. I saw her nudging one of the new stable hands when he was trying to do some work. I don't think she felt he was doing it quite right."

I settled into the couch, leaning back against the pillows and letting my mother's warm words wash over me. It reminded me of the home I'd used to have, how we'd worked in the stable together and mucked out the stalls. I could almost hear the whicker of the horses as they talked back and forth, dust and bits of straw floating in the air. It was hard, dirty work but I missed it anyway.

"Are you okay, Honey?" I heard her ask, jolting me out of my thoughts. "You're awful quiet."

"I'm fine Mom. Just feeling a little nostalgic right now. Missing you and the horses."

"You can come back anytime, you know. This is your home."

I took a deep breath, wishing I could give in to the little girl part of me that wanted to do exactly that. Run home and let Mommy take care of everything.

"I can't Mom, you know that. Me being there puts you at risk and I'm not willing to do that. Besides, Dad's sent me some guests for right now, so I've got to play the good hostess to them. Keep them out of trouble and all that." I tried to keep my response light, hoping that a little humor would take away some of the sting from my refusal to come home.

She sighed into the phone. I could picture her on the other end, one arm wrapped around her middle, a solo hug for comfort, teeth chewing on her bottom lip. It was how she'd always looked when she'd been missing someone. Missing my father.

"So," she said haltingly. "How's your Dad? Is he okay?"

I thought quickly, knowing Angus wouldn't want me to tell her the absolute truth. "Yeah, he's fine. Missing you, wishing he could be there, knowing he can't. Same as always."

She was quiet on the other end. Then, "Will you tell him something for me?"

"Of course, Mom."

"Tell him I," she paused for a second. "Just tell him none of this is his fault. He never wanted to listen to me when I tried to say that to him before, but it's the truth. He blames himself for me being sick and losing your brother, but none of us knew exactly what was happening." My eyes teared up as I listened to her, feeling how alone she was there without us. She caught her breath. "I wish he could forgive himself."

I nodded, then realized how silly that was. She couldn't see me, but I couldn't think of any words to say into the silence between us. We finally just whispered our love to each other and ended the call. I sat on the couch for a few minutes more, letting the quiet dark settle comfortably around me.

When I heard the long low bark from Moose signaling he and Cal were home again, I wiped away the tears on my face. I opened the door, Moose shooting by me to take a long drink from his water dish. Callum was breathing hard, but he pulled me gently out of the kitchen.

"Are you okay?" he asked. "Did something happen while we were gone?"

I wrapped my arms around my middle. "It's fine. I talked to my mom. Never an easy conversation. Things are complicated."

"Ah, yes." He didn't sound surprised, which made me curious.

"Have you met my mother?"

"No, I haven't. But your father loved to talk about his time with her. I feel like I know her. At least a little bit."

I wanted to ask him for details, find out what stories Angus had shared with him. But I didn't. I was emotional enough already. Instead, I chose to go upstairs to my room, where I could miss my family without anyone watching me.

Chapter Nineteen

LIVING ALONE, routine had been my friend. A comfort. Wake up, work, train, eat something. Then back to bed. Wake up the next day and do it all over again. And again. Until the days ran into weeks and I couldn't remember the last time I'd seen someone face to face.

Now, my comfortable routine had been upended and I was fighting the urge to scream. It was starting to feel like the only time I could manage to be alone was when I excused myself to go to the bathroom or take a shower. And if that took too long, Moose was pawing at the door, anxious for me to finish up and join the world again.

Then there was Cal. He was taking up too much space. That's the only way I could describe it. It wasn't him, but his presence. How he insisted on making me food, sitting down with me to eat, sparring when I needed a tough workout. He was carving out a place in the life I'd built. A life that didn't have room in it for other people.

As the days wore on and the badness Miss Tilly had predicted never showed up at the door, the hold I had on my feelings slipped. I began snapping at things more and more often. Dumb things, really; a pan left out or a piece of dog food crunching under my feet. They were reminders that my home wasn't just my home anymore. Which scared me. Because routine is a distraction too. You don't realize how lonely you are until someone forces companionship into your life, which makes you realize you don't want to be lonely again. Even though it's inevitable, and eventually you'll have to say goodbye to someone who laughed at your jokes and didn't care if you turned the music up when you needed to drown out the world. The moment when you look down and acknowledge the warm lump of canine covering your feet on a cold night can't stay forever.

Instead of talking about it, I threw myself into anything that kept me busy. And if it kept Moose and Cal at a distance, that worked too. I'd thought I was managing pretty well. Until the day Cal interrupted my knife practice.

"Okay," Cal said. "That one was a little too close."

"Well, it just proves you should be more careful about surprising me when I'm working on my knife throwing."

"That doesn't mean you should throw it at my head."

"And you shouldn't sneak up on me."

"I wasn't sneaking. I called your name three times."

I stomped away from him, yanking my knives from

where I'd embedded them in the target. It also gave me a chance to avoid his eyes. "Didn't hear you."

"That's a lie," he shot back.

"No, it's not." I fished around for something. "You're stealthy. And I was focused on what I was doing."

He didn't respond to that and when I turned around to face him, I wasn't happy to see him leaning against the back wall, silently laughing.

"What's so funny?" I tried to hide my need to fidget by spinning the knives through my fingers, working on my balance and control.

Now his laughter rolled out. "This is what's funny. It's like we're having our first fight."

"No, we're not." I ground the words out, my jaw clenched.

"Yes, we are. I don't know why, but we're definitely having our first fight."

"A fight would indicate we're a couple. Which we are not. We're a group. A group stuck living together in a house."

"And there it is. Finally, you're admitting what this is all about."

I shook my head, shouldering past him in an attempt to end the conversation. He grabbed my wrist, lightly, but it was enough to stop me.

"You know you shouldn't touch me." I pulled my hand away from him. "I don't want to talk about this right now, Cal."

"I think you need to. Something's bothering you and my

guess is it has a lot to do with the fact that Angus dumped us on you. You're feeling encroached upon and trying to reassert yourself."

I tried to argue with that but couldn't come up with anything in response. I slumped down to the floor, letting my head bump against the basement wall. "How did you come up with that?"

"Was I right?" he asked, a little too happily. "Did I figure it out?"

"Wait, you're happy about this?"

"A little. I've spent a lot of time researching relationships. It's good to see I've learned something."

"Research? Are you talking about the romances you read?" I snorted. "I don't think those count as legitimate research."

"Hey, I'm reading for a purpose. And it paid off. Plus, you're not mad anymore."

I tried to find the energy to yell at him, but it was all too ridiculous. I started laughing instead. "Fine. You win. For now."

He grinned at me from his spot by the wall. "Glad I got you laughing. But I think it would be a good idea for me to start taking Moose out on runs regularly. Hounds need a chance to burn off excess energy and frankly, you've been feeding him a lot. Plus, that should give you some time to yourself when you need it."

I stared at him. "You're joking right? Are you trying to win some award?"

He played innocent. "All I'm trying to do is my job. Which is to take care of you." He smiled and nodded at the far wall. "Now, I'm going to get out of your way and let you kill that target a few more times."

CHAPTER TWENTY

"SHAKE IT OFF, Delaney," I muttered to myself. "You need to know what's going on." I picked up my phone, placing the call I'd been delaying. When the line was picked up, I was ready.

"Hello, Ma'am," I said sweetly into the phone, not hiding the Texas drawl I'd picked up in my years living there. "I was hoping to speak with one of the men there in your office. Do you think you can help me?" I poured some magic into that question, letting it twine with my words and my voice. My goal was to soften her up, encourage her to share information with me. In the end, she wouldn't even remember our conversation. Assuming I did this the right way.

"I hope I can help you, sweetheart. Who're you looking for?"

"Detective Bishop. Torren Bishop."

I heard the hesitation before she answered. "Oh, I'm

sorry. He's not here." A significant pause punctuated her next words. "He's away right now. Vacation."

"Oh, no. He said I should call if I needed his help. I don't know what else to do." There was a little more push behind that statement, a little more sugar added to the mix with a hint of fear in my voice. I tried not to overdo it, worried she'd get suspicious and my attempt to influence her over the phone wouldn't work.

"You all right, honey? If you need some help, we can get someone to you."

Damn it. I'd pushed a little too hard and now she was worried. I wanted her sympathy. I didn't want the cavalry coming.

I backed off a little bit, draining away some of the magic I'd wrapped into my words. "No, I'm fine. For now. I just needed to talk with him and this was the number I had."

"Are you one of his girls?" she asked, cautiously.

Now, that was interesting. "One of his girls? I'm not sure what you mean." I let uncertainty creep in, unsure of exactly how much would give me the desired result. Winning someone over when you can't see them in front of you is harder than you'd think. And this wasn't something I practiced.

"The girls he's been helping. Or trying to help." She paused again, and when she continued, it was like she was trying to find a way to say things delicately after looking over her shoulder for anyone who might be listening. "He finds ways to get them out of the situations they're in. Through no fault of their own, of course," she added hastily at the end. "He gets them back to their families if they want. Or to a safe place."

Finally, something I could work with. "Yes, Ma'am, I'm one of those girls he offered to help. I'm safe now but there's another girl I know. He might be able to help her." I focused on the worry I felt for this imaginary girl, layering it on top of fear. My throat was going to be sore by the time this phone call was over with.

"He'd been working too much, he really needed some time off. But he'd want you to have a way to contact him while he's away." I heard her rummaging through a drawer before she came back on the line. "Here it is." I scribbled down the numbers as she read them off.

"Thank you, Ma'am. I truly appreciate this. My friend really needs his help."

"No need to call me Ma'am. Tausha will do just fine, honey. If you ever need anything and can't reach Torren, you call me. I'll get a message to him somehow. After the way he lost his sister, he's really thrown himself into helping other girls like her. I'm glad he got to you before something bad happened."

"Oh," I said. The shock of this revelation raced through me. "Did she die?"

"Poor thing was murdered. When he found out, I was so worried about him. Didn't think he'd ever find a way to get over it. Cassie was all he had, you know."

I didn't have to fake the shock that colored my voice now. "I didn't know that. He never mentioned it."

Tausha continued. "Since then, he's been helping girls like her when he can, trying to make something good out of this awfulness. He checks in with me every once in a while. Do you want me to give him a message?"

This I absolutely had to get right. I closed my eyes, replacing my sweet drawl with a heavy dose of steely intent. "No Tausha. I don't want you to give him a message. I want you to forget this phone call. Completely. Go to your car, get some lunch and when you return to your desk, you won't remember we ever spoke." I ended the call with those instructions.

Stunned, I sat at my desk, phone in my hand while my mind whirled through the details. He'd lost a sister, tried to help other women like her. I started biting at the rough edge of one of my fingernails, then forced myself to stop. Chewing on my nails was a bad habit that always showed itself when I was nervous or trying to solve a problem. With the additional women showing up dead after I'd supposedly killed the murderer, Torren was not going away. Newt's most recent message was that he hadn't found anything to reverse the binding we'd accidentally created. Torren had tried calling me multiple times, but I refused to speak with him. Having learned this information, though, I knew that Torren would never leave if he thought I was at risk, Bound or not.

CHAPTER TWENTY·ONE

I HATE TO run. It's painful and I can never seem to get enough oxygen. Watching Moose and Cal lope off together made me wish I could revel in it the way they did. But the time alone would be nice, and I appreciated Callum suggesting it. Having the house to myself for even a little while felt freeing.

I was going over my notes on the final items that needed to be done for the foundation's next event when I heard something outside. Sometimes, if the wind blew just right, tree branches would scrape against the wood shakes on the roof. I always tried to keep the trees trimmed because that sound grated on my nerves, making me think of claws scraping bones clean. An old childhood nightmare. I ignored it and kept working. A tickling itch tripped across my stomach, and I scratched at the skin, irritated by the distraction.

Focused on everything I had to get done, I jumped when I heard the back door slam shut. My arm jerked in surprise and knocked the paperwork I'd been reviewing off the desk. I was scrambling around on the floor, trying to put everything back in the right order when I heard the scraping sound again. Louder. From my kitchen.

I stayed on my knees, willing my heart to slow its sudden racing and calm my pulse.

I tried to reason with myself, to remember that my wards were strong enough to keep anything unwanted out. Then I froze. I couldn't remember when I'd last charged the stones. I should've checked them when I watched Moose and Cal take off on their run. But with the security of their company, I'd grown lazy and made myself an obvious target.

Dirty feet appeared in my line of sight. Long nails tapped against the floor's wood planks with each step and the muscled calves I could see were hairless, covered only by mottled gray skin. There was a rusty laugh that made my stomach twist with fear. It was a laugh that had tasted pain before and found it delicious.

"Come out, come out pretty girl. Come on out and play." The voice was gravelly, neither male nor female. It grated on me, rubbed my ears raw. "Come out, come out little one. Daddy's gone away."

Sudden realization hit me. I knew I was in trouble. The sing-song rhyme told me I had a Proles Demon in my house. They preferred to dine on children, using simple songs to lead their prey away until they could snatch them up with no one to see. They enjoyed causing fear, liking the flavor it added to the meat. But the reality was, they'd eat anything. Even me.

On the plus side, I wasn't a child. I knew what I was dealing with and I wasn't too afraid to fight back. I stood up, determined to face this threat head on. Long, snarled brown hair with streaks of rust hung in lank layers around a face dominated by perfectly round coal dark eyes. Cold and hungry. Those eyes were trained on me, unblinking. Lips pulled back from sharp teeth in a mockery of a smile as a hand with long claws reached out to me.

"Found you, found you pretty girl. Now it's time to play. Found you, found you, now your Daddy's gone away." The song was intended to lure children, trick them into trusting the image in front of them. But the glamour this demon could wear didn't appear to me. I could see the truth of what this creature was. Dirty and whipcord thin, unblinking eyes locked on me. Hungry, ready to rip me apart and swallow me down piece by piece. Clammy sweat trickled down my back, but if I was going to die, I had no intention of going quietly.

When the Proles Demon decided to strike, it came at me shockingly fast. One moment we faced each other across my living room, the couch a barrier that gave me some small sense of security. The next, it had crossed the space in a weird scuttling crouch that seemed impossible and slashed at my stomach in an instant. I dodged away from the claws, sliding to the left and swinging a haymaker at its jaw before it could change direction and come at me again. My fist connected, and I felt the satisfying vibration travel up my arm. The Proles snarled as it shook its head, turning toward me and moving more cautiously as it reevaluated me and my ability to cause it pain.

I backpedaled, keeping just the right distance between us, knowing I wouldn't be able to box my way out of this fight. But I could buy myself a little time. When it crouched to come at me again, I feinted with my right and caught it when it tried to shrink away from the punch, my left hook shocking it again, knocking it off balance. I wanted to create more room to maneuver so I kicked out, my right foot catching it square in the midsection and pushing it back. I was starting to breathe harder now, though, the adrenaline rushing through me. I knew I couldn't keep this up so when it came at me again, I dove to the right, letting my momentum carry me forward in a roll and then back to my feet, snatching the fireplace poker as I came up and swinging it at my attacker. I was rewarded by a meaty thump and a shrill shriek as I connected with its rib cage this time. I backed away, wanting to move toward escape or at least the basement where I would have a real weapon at hand. If I survived this battle, I promised myself I would start hiding the damn things everywhere, just in case. I might even consider listening to my father and start carrying them on me all the time.

The creature followed my every move, staying just out of reach and regarding me with a little more respect than it had before. There was a distinct hunger in its eyes. Blood lingered at the corner of its mouth and it smacked its lips. The weapons I'd been training with weren't at hand and I'd happily sent my guardians off on a run, probably with this demon outside watching. I'm sure I looked like an easy meal. The idea that it thought I was a simple snack waiting to happen made me mad. So, I poked the demon. With the poker.

I followed that up with a little more bravado, which I was willing to fake. "You want to eat, you're going to have to work a little harder than that."

The Proles circled me, and I followed, never exposing my back, both of us looking for the right opportunity to strike. I kept the poker primed, ready to block and attack, so when the demon tried to drive toward me, I was ready and swung it. Connected again. This time on its left wrist, which twisted at a painful angle with an audible crack. The creature hissed and drew back, drawing its hand up to its mouth and sucking at the blood that welled up through the broken skin. A stone gray tongue bobbed out, cleaning up the viscous fluid. Licking its wound. I swallowed against the revulsion I felt and stepped further back toward the kitchen, to a doorway I could slam and lock, precious moments where I could make a run for a real weapon.

The unexpected knock at my front door caught my

attention for only a brief second. But the small break in concentration was enough for the Proles and it grabbed for me in that instant of distraction. I darted back to avoid being caught, but strong fingers wrapped around my arm, the sharp claws digging in at my wrist, peeling off the skin as I was yanked toward the demon. I screamed and pulled back, losing my footing on the rug and tumbling to the ground. The Proles fell on top of me and it shrieked, sounding triumphant. I held the snapping mouth away from me, shoving up against the bony chin, ignoring the pain that blazed up my arm, the blood trickling from it as the talons dug in again.

Baring its teeth, fetid breath hitting me full on, the Proles giggled and began to sing again. "Have you, have you, pretty girl, Daddy's gonna pay. Have you, have you little one, now Daddy's gone away. Eat you, eat you, pretty girl, then Daddy cannot stay. Eat you, eat you, Daddy's got to pay."

I struggled, keeping my arms locked to hold the Proles away from me. I fought to pull my legs up to get some leverage, but the demon kept them pinned down, the weight of its body hard to combat. I screamed my frustration as the muscles in my arms started to shake. Vaguely, I heard the sound of wood shattering in the background but didn't look away from the snarling mouth above me. A thunderous growl shook the air and Moose came barreling into the room, sliding on the wood floors until he could regain control of himself. His launch forward propelled him onto the back of the Proles, the weight of his landing crushing down on me, driving the air from my lungs. The demon shrieked, its shrill voice drilling through my ears as my Hound's teeth sank in deep. He dragged the demon backwards. Claws cut even deeper into me as the creature futilely tried to keep its hold on my arm.

Callum came running into the room, Torren right behind him. Cal pointed at me and I dimly heard him say, "Stop her bleeding." Then he turned away from me to face the Proles, which struggled to get away from my Hound, whose jaws were locked tight on it. "You will tell me why you're here!" The command magic in his voice was unmistakable.

Torren reappeared in front of me, towels clutched in his hands, eyes wide and wary. He helped me up enough that I could lean back against the wall and then began to apply pressure to the wounds on my arm. I bit my lip, battling against the pain and the dizziness washing over me. It felt like I was burning from the inside, shards of glass lodged under my skin, intent on carving their way out of me. I wanted to drift off into a haze, so I wouldn't see or feel what was happening, but then the pain would spike and pull me back to awareness. I began to be afraid, really for the first time, that this is how my end would come. Taken down by a demon that hunted children. I didn't have the energy to stop the shaky laughter that worked its way out of me at the thought.

"Hells. Angus is really going to kill me after this." I started to shake, every muscle in me quaking, out of my control.

Torren looked at me, concern written clearly on his face. He looked back at Cal and Moose, in his full Hell Hound form, and the captive writhing on the floor. His breath caught, and I heard him whisper, "What the hell is that thing?" A simple question but I couldn't answer him. It took everything I had to hold myself together.

Cal was standing straight, taller than he'd ever seemed before, and his voice boomed in the small space. "You will tell me why you are here and who sent you!"

The Proles froze in its effort to claw at my Hound, the words pouring from Callum's mouth holding it in place. I heard the sing-song I'd come to hate reply. "Pretty girl, little girl, Daddy's gone away. Pretty girl, lonely girl, her Daddy's got to pay. Pretty girl, little girl, His power's gone away. Pretty girl, tasty girl, Man's given me to play."

The scene before me slowly faded, shades of black filtering around the edges. It happened in slow motion, the darkness seeping into my vision, narrowing it down until the only thing I could see was the bone gray of the demon's naked leg, shining like moonlight was hitting it. The brightness of it hurt my eyes and I closed them against it. I gave in to the darkness and let it lift me away, the pain dimming to nothingness.

Until it flared again and I was forced to open my eyes. Cal was above me, fear flashing in his eyes. They stood out to me, surrounded by a halo of rosy gold hair. If I looked closely, I could see the gold of his hair mirrored in the center of his eyes, eyes that I was sure would burn with flame if he let them. He was fiercely beautiful, like a warrior and angel were mixed up together into this one person. He called my name, loud in the suddenly strange silence. Something in me recognized it wasn't the first time he'd said my name, trying to pull me back to consciousness. I closed my eyes again and Cal pushed against my wrist, digging his fingers into the open wound, forcing me even further back to awareness.

I couldn't scream, but a groan escaped me, and I made a feeble attempt to pull away from his touch. He held on tight, a bleak smile on his face, confirmation he was intent on me being conscious even though I knew he hated to do it this way.

"Good. You're back," he said, so softly I could barely make out the words. Or maybe that was my brain processing things too slowly.

"You're pretty, you know." Hearing myself, I giggled a little, wondering at the things I was thinking and saying.

He shook his head, a small grin appearing briefly. "So, the girls tell me," he said dryly. Then he focused on me, his face worried and filled with some pain I didn't understand. "Laney, I've got to treat your wound right away. The claws of a Proles are filthy. Poisonous. If we don't do something now, it will fester, and you could die." He paused, but then said grimly, "This is going to hurt."

"Of course it is," I whispered, my mouth dry. Pounding feet sounded as Torren came into the room, a small leather bag clutched tightly in his hand. He shoved it at Cal, who looked away from me only for a second to take hold of it. Then he locked his eyes with mine, warmth flowing from his hand into mine and a tingling began where his skin touched mine. It felt good, drowning out the pain for a brief second.

He broke our connection too soon and I closed my eyes, needing rest and strength. I heard him tell Torren, "You'll have to hold her down." Moose whined in the background, and I felt the air around me move as Torren slid down beside me, helping me to lay down and propping something soft under my head. Then his strong hands came down on my shoulders. He whispered something over and again, but I couldn't make out the words. They reminded me of prayers I'd heard somewhere before and wanted to laugh. Praying over the body of the Devil's daughter. Who'd have ever thought things would come to this?

I opened my eyes one last time. I saw Torren's face, rigid with fear. His eyes were closed, and his lips moved in steady rhythm. Cal was on my left, dust falling from his hands onto the wrist where the claws had cut the deepest. The dust sparkled in the dim light, almost beautiful, a silvery arc suspended in the air as each mote fell toward me. One of them drifted down, landing on my skin and flared, brilliant. It was followed by its mates, thousands of blinding little pinpoints as they touched me and then disappeared, leaving a gentle numbness behind. I floated contentedly for a moment before the burning started, brutal and incessant, tearing through my skin and the muscles underneath, joining with my blood and traveling through my veins. It rode the wave within my body, pumped further and further with every beat of my heart. My legs kicked at the floor and I screamed, twisting against the weight holding me down. I couldn't stop myself, even as the pressure on my shoulders increased and I felt the warmth of my Hound as he laid his heavy body across my legs, helping to keep me in place.

It continued on, more spikes of pain, more fire spreading through me. My screams grew hoarse and I tired of fighting against the weight of those hands and bodies. My cries turned to whimpers and this time, I welcomed the weightless feeling of unconsciousness when it came and gave in to it.

Chapter Twenty·Two

I awoke in my own bed. My left arm was wrapped in bandages and it ached when I tried to lift it. I struggled upright and saw Moose laying at my feet, blankets scratched up into a bed. Even back in his smaller form, his heat permeated the covers and I smiled at the simple comfort his presence gave me. He lifted his head at my movement and whined a little, then crawled on his belly until he was beside me and I was able to lay my undamaged hand on his head. We both slept that way for a little while longer, soothing each other as best we could.

When I woke a second time, Moose was gone and Cal had taken his place, sitting on the mattress next to me and checking my pulse. Seeing my open eyes, he offered me a drink of the cold water he'd brought in with him. I swallowed it down, recognizing the soreness in my throat as evidence of how long I'd screamed. I drank the whole glass and he set it back down before he said anything at all.

"You're even more of a fighter than I thought. You gave all of us a tough time last night."

I watched him, seeing the tension in his shoulders and the tightness of his jaw. His eyes were tired, and pieces of his hair stuck up at odd angles, making me think he'd run his fingers through it over and over. His hands were gentle as he checked my wound, unwinding the bandages until my skin was bare. He held my arm tenderly, carefully turning it from side to side. I could see the thick, twisting lines of scars that hadn't been there before. Skin that should have been torn apart and gaping open had sealed, leaving only the ridged traces as evidence of what had happened.

"How did you do that?" I asked him, breathless at the thought of what he'd somehow forced my body to do in a matter of hours.

He shrugged, like it wasn't all that extraordinary. "Battlefield healing. You needed it. Definitely wasn't easy but we got the job done."

"It hurt. A lot."

"I know. I'm sorry for that but there was no way to make it easier. Anything else wouldn't have acted fast enough. It was the only way."

He winced as his fingers feathered over the scars. Watching him, I could see he hadn't wanted to cause me pain. But knowing him as I did by now, I also knew he'd do it again without question if required. I was just as determined to never need that again in the future.

"You should teach me how do this." I tried a grin. "I want to be able to repay this favor in the future, you know."

He seemed to relax at the teasing note in my voice. "It was silver nitrate. Specially prepared, fast acting amplified with some magic. I pushed it even further with some of my energy, shoved that into you every chance I got."

I caught my breath at that. The one thing I wanted no one to ever do, to be forced to share their energy with me, to peel off parts of their soul to sustain me. The thing I'd left the world behind to avoid. He'd done that to save me.

I looked away from him, out the window to the bright white clouds I could see. I kept my gaze there, even as I said, "I wish you hadn't done that. I hate that you were forced to."

His fingers were firm on my cheek, turning me to face him. His voice was serious. "Listen to me. I wasn't forced to do anything, Laney. It was a choice I made when it was needed. Someday you'll see these abilities you have as the gifts they can be. You'll learn to accept them and find a way to make them work for good. I know you enough already to recognize that." When I opened my mouth to argue, he stopped me with a shake of his head. "I was happy to share myself with you that way. Don't treat it as a hateful thing—the fact that we are able to do that for each other can be something so wonderful."

I protested. "I can't do anything for you. All I can do is take. I don't want to be someone who steals from people, who takes what they can't afford to give."

He wrapped his fingers through mine. "Who says you can't do anything for me? You don't know yet, because you haven't tried. Like I told you, once you find a way to accept what you can do, I believe you'll learn to control it. Maybe then, you'll find you can share yourself in the same way. And you'll really be able to return the favor."

He smiled, and I felt myself warming up, unable to stop myself. We sat together for a moment, his fingers twined with mine, just smiling at each other until a knock at the open door fractured our quiet moment and we saw Torren standing there, watching us.

He stayed at the threshold, but looked to Cal. "Did you tell her yet?"

"He told me," I answered back, determined to be included in this conversation.

Torren cocked a brow at me. "Everything?" he shot back.

I looked between them, sensing something I didn't have enough information to understand. When the silence lengthened, harsh and tight, I broke it with a sigh. "Fine. What else do I need to know?"

Cal stayed where he was beside me, but Torren stepped into the room, closing the distance that separated us. "You were dying," he said, spitting it out like the words tasted bad. Bitter.

I nodded. I'd already guessed this, based on how much

blood I'd probably lost and the tense atmosphere when I'd finally come back to myself.

"You were dying and suddenly, I couldn't breathe. It was like being sucked down a hole where there's no air and no light and there's nothing you can do to stop it. Until he grabbed me and shocked the hell out of me." He pointed at Cal, the accusation hanging unspoken. But I waited. If there was a question, he was going to have to ask it.

Finally, he broke. "Well, are either of you going to tell me what is happening?"

Cal stood up and started to leave the room, but I put a hand on his arm, silently asking him to stay. He nodded once but didn't sit back down next to me. He leaned up against the wall instead, giving Torren and me space to discuss the situation. His hands looked relaxed, one resting on his thigh as his foot propped him up and the other in the front pocket of his jeans. But I could sense that was a facade. He was ready to launch forward if need be, to get between me and the possible danger when Torren realized what had happened between us.

I patted the now empty spot on the bed next to me, reaching out a hand to him. I could understand his reluctance to sit in the precise spot that Cal had vacated, but I also knew he needed to be close to me right now. I was going to do this right. Even if it broke his heart.

He paused, weighing my offer and then stepped across the empty space between us, sliding onto the softness of my bed and the warmth it promised, unconsciously leaning a little of his weight against me. He sat there, his eyes on me, waiting.

"The day you asked me to meet you because you needed to show me the pictures of those other girls." I looked at his face, to confirm I had his attention, and then forged ahead. "You grabbed me, and you kissed me." I said it quietly, no emotion, no anger. These were mere facts. "And something happened when you did that."

I held my breath, wondering if I should continue. But he broke in, nodding his head. "I felt it. It was a shock, like you get when there's static electricity and you touch something. That's what you're talking about?"

I nodded. "That was it. I was surprised by what you did. I wasn't prepared. Normally, when I'm with people, I have my defenses up. I shield myself from others. But when you did that, well, I was wide open. And so were you. So, we kind of connected." I felt like I was doing a bad job with this, wanting to find the right words to explain all this to someone who had no concept this could even happen. "I'm sorry. I've never had to actually explain this to anyone before. Do you understand what I'm talking about?"

"Chemistry?" he asked, quirking a corner of his mouth.

His attempt at humor worked. I laughed in spite of everything. "Something like that, I guess." But the reality was sobering, and I needed to help him understand. "But it's deeper, really. That moment, when you felt that charge between us..." *Here it comes.* "We became connected at a soul level. And now, without meaning for any of this, we're tied together. Wrapped up. Stuck." I spread my hands in what I knew was a useless gesture, and could feel his eyes boring into me, burning a hole into the top of my head because I couldn't look at him while I said this. "I'm sorry this happened to you. So very, very sorry."

He waited, still as a statue, so I shut my mouth, giving him a chance to process everything. We hung there, the three of us, in this odd triangle, all of us letting the silence stretch while something bigger than each one of us happened outside our control.

His voice, when it came, felt brittle to my ears. "You're serious? Really? Because I'm starting to think you're both playing some weird game." He looked back and forth between Cal and me. There was nothing either one of us could say. Anything I could offer would sound like feeble protests. He had to come to this understanding on his own. And before that, he would be angry. Hurt. He moved suddenly away from me, jumping up and pacing the length of my room. Cal remained in his chosen position against the bedroom wall, but his eyes tracked Torren.

"So what, you're a vampire or something? A demon soul sucker?"

There it was. The anger he needed to vent. I stayed quiet. Letting him work through each layer, prepared to bear the weight of it all as he worked his way through it.

"I'm like, food for you? What is this? You just lure guys in and trick them into falling for you, then force them to be your slave for the rest of their lives? How many other guys have you done this to? How many?"

He was yelling now, fists clenched, a vein standing out along the side of his neck, but there was an undercurrent of desperation I could hear beneath the venom he was spouting at me. He knew this was serious, that we weren't playing any games, and he was scared. He had every right to be afraid. I'd been draining his life away on the floor of my living room and hadn't even known it. Only Cal's intervention had saved us both. Hells, even I was afraid right now.

And it was Cal who saved us again. His long body uncoiled from the wall slowly, so as not to startle either of us, and he stepped over to Torren, who had started to shake. Resting his hand on Torren's shoulder, he said quietly, "This wasn't anyone's fault. You surprised her, and she wasn't prepared. She's been living out here by herself, trying to keep this very thing from happening. If you really look at her, you'll see she's just as frightened by all this as you are. She's terrified you'll be hurt. It's okay to be angry and afraid but direct it where it needs to be."

"And where is that?"

"At whoever sent that Proles Demon here for Laney. If she hadn't been hurt, the connection between you wouldn't have activated the way it did. We'd have had time to work this out more and find some answers. But somebody out there didn't want us to have that kind of time."

"You think I was set up?" I asked, breaking into the conversation between them.

Cal looked at me and nodded. "The Proles said you were promised to it by someone. There was no name, just a man, but it was clear that it was sent here to attack you."

"And once a Proles has a target, they hunt it down. Never stopping. Until they get what they want." I remembered my lessons with Newt about the types of demons, information he felt was essential I learn. Not my favorite subject, but at least I'd retained some of what he'd been trying to teach me.

"It said something else about you, Laney. About why it might want you dead." Cal's voice was serious, his words heavy with an emotion I couldn't identify.

"What did it say?" I asked, afraid of what it might be.

Cal's eyes were sad as they met mine. "She lives, we die. She lives, the world will cry."

Torren scoffed. "I heard that too, but it's just nonsense. It could mean anything."

Cal shook his head. "No. I held that Proles under a command. It truly believed every word it was telling me. It was sent here for Laney, because someone believes that if she lives, the world will end . . . at least for demons."

I forced myself out from under the blankets, standing up on unsteady feet, realizing suddenly that I had very little on and what I was wearing was not what I'd picked out earlier in the day. A problem I didn't have time to deal with at the moment. "You think I'm going to be the end of demons?" I asked.

"I didn't say I think that. I said that's what the Proles believed. That's what it was told by whoever sent it after you." He started to say something else, but stopped himself, his lips pinched together.

"What? What did you just think of?" I demanded.

His answer came as a whisper. "There have always been rumors that some Proles can glimpse the future."

Cold began to creep from my stomach up to my throat. I didn't want this to be true. I'd always tried my best to stay hidden when I could, and now, attention was about to fall on me in the very worst way.

"Cal, if other demons hear this, they'll come after me. After all of us." I waved my hands frantically at the group of us, including Moose in the gesture. And I realized something else. "My Dad. We have to call my Dad. And Newt. They need to know what happened."

This was all apparently too much for Torren. "Wait a minute, your dad? I thought your father died in some airplane crash. Now you're saying we have to give him a call. What, is he a demon too?" He started to laugh at the idea, almost like he expected us to join in. When neither Cal nor I said anything, he deflated, the look on his face incredulous. "He is? A demon?"

I started to explain but was cut off as the pressure

heralding my father's impending arrival began to build up, the heat filling the small room quickly and the scent of brimstone rising until there was an audible pop and a flare of light. When the brightness faded, Angus stood there, every inch the arrogant rock star and enraged father.

CHAPTER TWENTY·THREE

I STEPPED FORWARD immediately, ready to bear the brunt of whatever he was planning to let loose on us. "Dad. I'm glad you're here." I was interrupted by Torren's sharp voice saying exactly the wrong thing.

"Speak of the Devil."

Angus turned his burning eyes on Torren, the flames chasing the dark centers evidence of how angry he really was. If you looked at them too long, they would pull you in and you'd forget everything. Those eyes could consume you and burn you alive.

"Careful what you call me, boy. You might not like what you get when I answer." His fury was almost visible, his words knife sharp. "Right now, you will call me Mr. Murphy. Or Sir. Anything else and I make no promises about your safety."

Then he pinned those eyes on me and I was rooted in

place by his power. Oh yes, he was pissed. And I was going to hear all about it.

"Callum. Please escort Mr. Bishop to the living room and keep him there. The Hound as well." His voice allowed no argument and Cal was wise enough to not even try. "My daughter and I have some things to discuss. Privately."

Torren tried to protest but Cal took him firmly by the arm and led him out of my room. I didn't know much about Cal's history, but I could tell he'd been around Angus long enough to know when retreat was the smartest move you could make. Getting Torren away from my father was the safest thing for everyone right now. Moose followed them out with a sad glance back at me.

When they'd left, Angus closed the door then returned his attention to me. The flames in his eyes were brighter now, swirling with his agitation. He pointed a finger at me and started to open his mouth, but I didn't let him say anything.

"Look, I know you told me to be careful and I was. I let Moose and Callum move into my home, just like you wanted. I even stayed away from Torren, but then he came out here anyway. And someone sent a Proles demon after me." The words raced out of me. I had to get them out before he tried to stop me. "From what they told me, I almost died. Which according to the Proles, could actually have saved the world. Since I'm the bringer of the Apocalypse. Or something like that." I sagged down into the chair someone had moved in while I was unconscious. It was embarrassing how fatigued I was after just a few minutes of standing.

Angus fumed quietly for a moment, running his hand through the mahogany curls he was known for. He'd always liked to tease me about our matching hair. All the different species of demons carried this mark in some way. Hells, even the Proles had streaks of rust in that matted mess I'd seen. Humans had long been suspicious of redheads. A superstition born of instinct. But I was the only one of his creations that was such a close copy. His hair, his coloring. His power.

"How did the Proles get into the house? How did it even get close enough to attack you?" Angus asked. He was speaking in that quiet, contained voice he only used when he was furious. It had always been a sign that I was truly, deeply in trouble.

Oh, this was not going to go well. "Um. Well, Cal and Moose went for a run and I wanted to stay here. When they left, I didn't think to check the wards around the house."

"So, the demon was able to walk right in." His voice was low and sharp. I would have almost preferred him to be yelling at me rather than hear the disappointment in his words.

"I'm sorry. It's not like I wanted a demon to come strolling into my house and try to make me a meal." I fought to keep the tears out of my voice and my eyes.

Angus sighed. "I thought you were smarter than that. That's all. You've been telling me all along how you can survive alone out here, how you can protect yourself without help. Yet you forgot something as basic and necessary as checking your wards."

I shrugged. "People forget things sometimes. All I can say is, I will try harder next time. And I will."

"I don't think you understand Delaney. You don't have a clue what it would do to me to lose you. And what about your mother? Even though she can't be with you, just knowing that you're alive in the world is more important to her than anything else. Losing you would break her. She's lost so much in her life already. I'm afraid she wouldn't survive if something happened to you."

I stared at him, dumbfounded and saddened. He was right. Not once had I thought of how my mom would be hurt if something happened to me. I'd separated myself from her to keep her safe in the first place. Again, my intentions had been good. But I hadn't seen the full picture.

"You meant well when you chose to leave," Angus said, startling me with his soft words, the familiar brogue coating them a comfort. "But that doesn't mean things will turn out the way you intend."

"So now you can read minds too?"

He chuckled softly. He pulled me up from the chair and wrapped me in his strong arms. "All I want to do is protect you, Delaney. You are the most amazing thing I've ever done. I need you alive. That's all. And I will do anything in my power to keep you safe."

"I never really thought of how you and Mom would feel if something happened. I mean, I know you both love me, but I never thought of it the way you just put it."

Angus hugged me even tighter, stroking my hair. "You're not a parent, honey. It becomes a whole different world once that happens. Trust me."

I relaxed against his warmth for a few minutes, knowing we both needed this. He felt strong and solid, holding me up against everything that seemed determined to knock me down. Angus let me rest there, allowing me to draw some strength from his presence.

"Laney love," he whispered into my hair, using my childhood nickname. "Please tell me you'll agree, now."

"Agree to what?" I asked, my voice soft.

"Let me place a piece of Hell inside you. We talked about it before, but it would help you in so many ways."

I reluctantly pulled away, shaking my head as I did. "I can't."

Angus grabbed my shoulders, holding me firmly in front of him. "This is important. You'd have easy access to your magic any time you needed it. You could pull right from me in an emergency."

I searched his face, seeing his need to keep me safe stamped on every feature. "I know what you're trying to do. I appreciate it, Dad. But I can't." I didn't know how to explain the fear constantly haunting me. I was his daughter, but I was human as well. A deep seated survival instinct told me that my humanity was the first thing I would lose if I gave in.

Silence stretched between us, his eyes locked with mine. "Think about it, please. There are benefits to this. And you'd never be cold again." He gave me a crooked grin and leaned in to kiss my forehead.

As he released me, I grabbed his hand. "Who is Callum? I can tell he doesn't want to talk about it but I need to know."

Angus gave me a pointed, direct look. "I'm not the one to ask about his secrets. All I will tell you is that he's someone I've known for a very long time and I trust him. With your life."

"This is information I need to have."

My father didn't answer. Instead, he stubbornly shook his head.

"I'm serious. I don't know how close I can let him get." This felt more awkward than I expected, but I had to know. "He had to work some healing on me while I was unconscious, gave me some of his own energy. I don't want him ruined because he's forced to be here with me. I need to know if that's a risk for him."

"He'll be fine. Any bond he forges with you will be of his own choosing."

"He's not human then. Which means he must be a demon."

Angus looked at me with an almost sad smile on his lips. "He's human enough. But he's Other too. Strong enough to resist you. If he wants to."

This was the Angus I knew best, talking in riddles and not answering simple questions. Not when he could throw you a puzzle and laugh while you struggled to find the answers. It always frustrated me.

"This is serious, Angus."

My father reached over and took my hand. "I'm being serious, Delaney. His is not a story for me to tell. Have a little faith. If you have questions, sit him down and talk to him. Maybe he'll give you the answers you're looking for. Stranger things have been known to happen."

I sighed, but it was clear that he wasn't going to be sharing anything else with me. Seeing that he'd won this battle with me, he nodded at the door. "I think it would be wise for us to go out there and continue our discussions with the gentlemen waiting on us. Before they come to blows."

I closed my eyes in frustration but knew he was right. He was no doubt able to sense what was happening out there, so if he thought they needed a distraction, we should provide one.

CHAPTER TWENTY·FOUR

WHEN WE WALKED into the living room, Moose was seated at Cal's feet, intent on the palpable tension between the two men. His rigid position relaxed a bit when my father cleared his throat, easily communicating that he was relieved to have someone else be responsible for whatever was about to happen here.

"So, gentlemen," Angus said, stepping between them. "The testosterone is so thick out here we can practically smell it. What seems to be the trouble?"

Torren clenched his fists at his sides but refused to say anything. Cal was the complete opposite, almost too relaxed, leaning back against the cushions. Underneath it all though, I knew he truly was ready for anything that might happen.

It was Cal who answered my father. "Torren feels I took advantage of Delaney while she was unconscious. Now that she's healed, he intends to defend her honor."

I saw my father's lips twitch up at one corner but other than that, he maintained a neutral expression.

"Ah, I see. Admirable. And how exactly did you take advantage of my daughter?"

"Her core body temperature was dropping quickly after she was hurt and I needed to bring it back up to facilitate the healing process. If I couldn't get her temperature to return to normal, I was afraid we might lose her completely." Cal kept his voice even, void of emotion, like he was reciting something he'd learned from a book.

"And you did that how?"

Torren broke in, anger coating every word. "He stripped off her clothes and carried her into the shower. He locked the door so I couldn't come in and keep an eye on what he was doing."

I felt myself flushing a bright red. That explained why I'd been wearing different clothes when I woke up. And why I wasn't covered in blood.

Angus was definitely enjoying himself. "Callum, I'm assuming that this was a hot shower and you were also unclothed?"

A brief nod was Cal's only response. Mine was to blush even more obviously than I had a moment ago. If my temperature had been too low before, now every inch of my skin felt embarrassingly hot.

Unlike Cal, Torren wasn't about to stay quiet. "He tried

to say that Delaney wouldn't have wanted me to see her like that. And when I still tried to get in there, that damn dog knocked me over and sat on me."

Nothing, it seemed, surprised my father, but I coughed out a laugh I couldn't hold in. The simple image of Moose sitting on Torren was hilarious, but I could understand his frustration. He'd been struggling with our bond in that moment and hadn't known what was going on. All he'd known was he needed to be with me. Even if it would've made everything worse.

Angus, however, wasn't as forgiving. "First of all, young man, you need to understand that damn dog is a Hound. One of my Hounds, in fact. And as such, he should be treated with the utmost respect. If he doesn't eat you, count yourself lucky." Moose cocked his head and curled his lip, showing his teeth, an action I interpreted as a warning. Angus then directed his attention back to Cal. "Knowing a little about the healing process, I believe that skin to skin contact is required. Am I correct, Callum?"

Cal nodded, starting to explain, but Torren interrupted him. "That's what he tried to tell me before he carted her off in there. And he said that he was less likely to be distracted since he'd already seen her in the shower before!"

I choked. I wanted the floor to open up and swallow me. The embarrassment was simply too much. But my father was in his element, loving every moment of the exchange, looking back and forth between the two of us. "Did he now?

Funny how no one mentioned that before. Well, Callum, please elaborate on that for us all. I'm very interested to hear how you managed to see my daughter in the shower. Naked."

Cal had the decency to at least look a little chagrined, but that was fleeting. He spread his hands. "Angus, it's not what you think. It was all a misunderstanding."

Angus quirked an eyebrow. "A misunderstanding that resulted in you seeing my daughter without her clothes on? I really do have to hear this." He was playing the role of protective father, but behind the stern face he was wearing I knew he was enjoying this enormously.

I stepped into the conversation. "It's your fault actually." His gaze shifted to focus on me as I continued. "When you sent Cal here and shoved him through the wards, I was in the shower. So of course, he showed up in the bathroom. That's how it happened." Looking at the men in front of me, I thought it best to add, "And that is ALL that happened."

Cal backed me up. "Exactly. She asked me to wait for her downstairs, and when she had dried off and dressed, she joined me here and we properly introduced ourselves. She showed me to the guest bedroom and that is where I spent the night." Then for good measure he said, "Where I have spent every night. Alone."

If dogs could laugh, I think Moose would have been rolling on the floor at the mess playing out in front of him. As it was, he had what must have been the Hound equivalent of a smile on his face, his tongue lolling out as he watched the exchanges between all three men. If Hounds really could talk, this one already had a million stories to share.

Angus was nodding, a glint in his eye belying the serious face he was trying to maintain. "Good to know. Sounds perfectly reasonable. Does that make you feel better Detective Bishop?"

"I don't like it, but if Delaney says that's the truth, I'll believe her."

All eyes were fixed on me. Thankfully, it felt like some of the heat-soaked flush I'd been overcome with before had faded slightly. I probably only looked bright pink instead of fire red. "It's the truth. Cal has been a gentleman the entire time he's been here, even when Angus dumped him in my bathroom." I glanced at Callum, hoping he'd understand that I wanted to leave the whole part about me seeing him in his nothings as something that didn't need to be discussed. The corner of his mouth went up, a small crooked smile acknowledging my message.

"Well, that settles it," Angus said brightly. "Now, let's tackle another difficult topic that we need to get out of the way." Turning to Torren, he said, "Did Callum tell you who I am?"

"I already know who you are. You're Angus Murphy. And you're supposed to be dead."

My father just waved his hand at that, shaking his head.

"No, no, no. Not what I asked you. Did Callum tell you who I am?"

Torren looked confused and uncomfortable. "He said you're really the Devil, that you created the identity of Angus Murphy so you could live on Earth for a while. And while you were living here, Delaney was born."

"As is the way of biology. And Lust," Angus interjected, waving Torren's words aside. "But the question is whether you believe what he told you or not?"

"Why would anyone believe that?" asked Torren.

A gleeful smile spread across my father's face and he stood up, rubbing his hands together like he was trying to warm them up or prepare for a magic trick. "Are you saying you need proof that I am who Callum says I am?"

Torren shrugged. "Honestly, I don't think there's anything you could do that would make me believe you're the Devil."

Joy radiated from my father. "Yes! Oh my, I have always loved the Doubters of this world so very much. You will be my very own Doubting Torren and shall be recorded in my Histories. This is going to be so much fun!" Pointing to Callum, he said, "Step over there and be ready to catch him when he falls. Delaney go on into the kitchen and get this young man a glass of water, and a shot of something strong. He's going to need it in a few minutes."

"Angus, please don't do this," I said, prepared to beg. Torren had been through enough already. Adding to it might rattle him so much he'd never recover.

My father turned his eyes on me. "Now Laney. It's time for you to leave the room. It's best we get this over with, so we can all move on to the important things."

I sighed, knowing I wasn't going to change his mind. When Angus wanted something, he was relentless. And he wanted Torren to see him for who he really was.

I heard the crackle of flames leaping up as I left the room. Heat erupted behind me but burned off quickly, leaving behind the brimstone scent I loved. It was like smelling birthday cake or fresh bread baking—so many happy memories were mixed up with it that I would never be able to let it go. It made me feel safe and content. One sniff and I was a little kid again, sitting in Daddy's lap with Mom across the way, all of us laughing as Dad conjured magical things and did tricks just to make us smile.

I heard Torren's loud gasp of shock and resisted the urge to go back in there. One thing I knew very well was that my father wanted me to see the face of Angus Murphy when I thought of him. Seeing his true form was simply not allowed. I filled a glass with cold water and poured some whiskey into another. When I moved into my home, Angus had brought me some Fireball Whiskey. He called it a housewarming gift, but I think he liked the devil on the bottle more than anything. He'd only had one shot that first night to toast my new home and never asked for another. The bottle had been sitting in the cabinet, untouched, since then. Good thing alcohol doesn't spoil. At least, I hoped it didn't. There was a loud grating sound from the living room that I recognized might have been an attempt at laughter but came out like two stones smacking against each other and reducing into pebbled gravel. Apparently, laughing wasn't exactly easy when my father wasn't in human form.

There was another flash of heat that I could feel even in the kitchen and then Dad's voice came to me again. "You should probably bring those drinks in, Delaney."

I walked in to the living room, seeing Torren's open-mouthed astonishment and Cal's contained laughter. I handed the drinks to Torren, watching carefully as he drank the shot of whiskey faster than I felt was safe. His hand was quivering a bit, but I pretended not to notice. He sputtered as the whiskey burned its way down his throat, but then washed it down with some water.

Trying to lighten the mood, I said, "Please, please tell me that at least he didn't brandish a pitchfork this time."

Angus tried unsuccessfully for an innocent face. "A pitchfork? My dear, you know me so much better than that. I'd never do something so expected."

I flopped down onto the couch next to him, sarcasm in my voice. "I suspect your pitchfork is the reason why I was only asked out once." I didn't say anything else, keeping the painful memory of that one date locked away. I didn't want to talk about it again so soon.

"All part of my fiendish plan," Angus said, laughing. He

grabbed my hand, holding it fondly for a moment with our fingers laced together before lifting it up into the light to examine the gleaming white scars that ran around my wrist and up onto my arm. His fingers traced the lines, as if trying to find a message written in them. Releasing me, he said, "You managed to do some very good healing with this, Callum. You've always been the best. I just hoped you wouldn't have a reason to use it here."

"I know, Sir. But I'm glad I was here when she needed me."

Angus nodded. "You know, these scars will be an easy way to identify Delaney once the rumors spread that she's been hurt. And the rumors will spread." His tone sounded worried and it made me wonder what things he still hadn't told me. "We'll have to find some way to disguise them." He whistled low and then stood up. "Now, I know too well the type of healing Cal did requires a lot of rest afterwards. So, I suggest all of you use this time to do exactly that. Detective Bishop, if you choose to stay, I expect you will be a gracious guest and do as you're asked. I understand your need to be close to Delaney right now, but you will honor the boundaries she puts in place. We're all too busy to play babysitter to you right now."

Torren nodded, watching as my father shook Cal's hand, then pulled me into a hug. With a quick kiss to my cheek, Angus popped out of my living room, the faint waft of char the only reminder he'd been there.

With my father gone, Torren recovered the ability to speak and turned wide eyes to us. "I don't believe it. Is the Devil really Irish?"

CHAPTER TWENTY·FIVE

I WASN'T SURE what to do with Torren for the night. It wasn't fair to kick Cal out of the room he'd been sleeping in and it was the only spare bedroom I had. For now, as worn out as we all were, Torren didn't object to sleeping on the couch. I think all that mattered to any of us was sleep. We'd deal with the rest of it in the morning.

Once it seemed like Torren was reasonably comfortable in the living room, I wished him a good night and plodded upstairs to get myself ready for bed. More than anything, I wanted to brush my teeth. After everything that had happened and the sleep I'd needed to properly heal, they were feeling filmy and gross. Scrubbing them clean was the only thing on my mind so I was off balance when I bumped into Callum in the hallway.

He steadied me, then pulled his arms away, stepping back to give me a little bit of space.

"Sorry about that, Laney. Didn't think you'd be up here quite so fast. Everything okay down there?"

I nodded. "I think so. It'll work for tonight at least."

"How are you feeling? Any pain or nausea?"

He sounded so professional in his concern. "I'm fine. Tired. Which I guess is probably normal after all we went through."

"Yeah, your body's been through the wringer. Get some rest tonight and I'll make sure you've got a good breakfast waiting when you get up. You'll probably be starving then. Appetite takes a little while to kick in after you start healing, but once it hits, you're going to want to eat just about everything."

He started to walk into his bedroom, but I stopped him with a touch on his arm. "Cal, I want to thank you for everything you've done to help me. I know you didn't want to come here in the first place, but obviously, I wouldn't still be here without you. And you managed the whole situation with Torren and Angus really well. Most people wouldn't have known what to do. Including me. So, thanks." I took a deep breath and let it out slowly, recognizing how hard it had been for me to admit I had needed his help.

I looked up to find his gaze intensely focused on me. "You're welcome, Delaney. Really." There was a husky quality to his voice when he said my name that made me almost uncomfortable, if only because I thought a part of me wanted it to mean more than it probably did.

"Okay, well, good night then." I started to turn away but then changed my mind and threw my arms around him in a quick, awkward hug. Then I rushed into my bedroom and shut the door without looking at him again.

When I woke in the morning, I was stiff and sore, but determined to face the problems in my home head on. I wanted battle armor. Best to make do with whatever was comfortable. I grabbed my favorite teal sweater and the most worn pair of jeans I had clean, slipping them on. The waistband gaped in the back, evidence of the fast healing of the day before. The mirror was no friend to me either, every bruise in high relief on my fair skin. Trying to cover them would be too obvious, so I settled for washing my face and dashing on a tiny bit of lip balm to help heal the cuts that were starting to sting.

Feeling as good as I possibly could after the previous day, I made my way downstairs. As promised, breakfast was waiting for me. Waffles and eggs were steaming and ready on the island while bacon sizzled on the stove. Cal watched over the meat and Torren was at the table. An uncomfortable silence reigned.

Might as well dive in. I sank down onto the seat across from Torren. "So, I think today we need to get your stuff moved out here and a proper bed set up. I don't expect you to sleep on the couch until this is all resolved, and it's only fair you have somewhere for your things. There's a small room upstairs that we should be able to fit a bed into for you."

Torren nodded. "Thanks Delaney. I appreciate it." Then he was back to drinking his coffee, his eyes studiously on the wood of the tabletop.

I turned to Cal, who had remained quiet while he finished preparing breakfast. Based on the amount of food I could see, it looked like he intended everyone should eat. I even suspected he'd made extra bacon for Moose, who was lurking under the table in anticipation of strategically dropped pieces.

"Smells good, Cal." My stomach grumbled loudly, and I added, "You're right. My appetite is definitely coming back. We'll need some food to get ready for the work ahead of us today. We've got to drive into Omaha, get Torren's stuff picked up, find a bed and get it set up out here before it gets too late."

"My stuff's in Hazelwood already," interjected Torren. As I turned back to him, he said, "I moved out to the bed and breakfast after we saw each other at the coffee shop." He paused, obviously uncomfortable. "I just felt like I needed to be closer to you."

"Okay," I said brightly, forcing cheerfulness in my voice. "That will make things a little easier. We can call Donna Kay and let her know you'll be checking out today. Then we'll pick up your stuff."

Neither Cal nor Torren said anything else, so I grabbed a plate and piled it high with food. I really was hungry, more than I could ever remember being, and everything smelled delicious. I wasn't going to pass this up. Not if I could help it.

Ignoring the tension in the air, I sat back down and dug in to my breakfast. Eventually, Cal and Torren both got plates of their own and joined me at the table, the sound of utensils scraping against the plates our only accompaniment. Moose was lingering by my feet, his head still under the table. I suspected more than a few small bits of bacon had found their way onto the floor, happily scavenged by the dog. If we could have managed some conversation, it might actually have been a pleasant meal.

The food disappeared with amazing speed. We cleaned up together, my lonely attempts to engage them in some discussion got simple sentence responses in return. I finally gave in and left the room, grabbing my phone and calling Donna Kay at the bed and breakfast. I let her know Torren was going to be checking out and I thought we'd be there soon to pick up his stuff. She said all he needed to do was sign the check-out paperwork. She'd have it printed up and ready for him.

Going back into the kitchen, I saw Moose and Cal walking a slow perimeter of the house, starting in the backyard and continuing around, clockwise, until they were out of sight as they passed to the front. Torren cleared his throat and when I turned my attention to him, said, "He's out checking the defenses with the dog. Said something about making sure the wards are in place and fully charged."

I nodded. "Probably smart. When we leave, I'll close the

wards but if there's a hole we need to mend, it's best we have that fixed ahead of time."

Torren's gaze was unsure, but he tried for a grin. "I, uh, have a lot to learn about things here."

I understood his confusion and even the worry I could detect below his words. "Hey, what you've been through and learned the past couple days would be a shock to anyone. Give yourself some time to adjust and you'll be fine."

His eyes were bleak. The shadow of unshaven growth on his jaw stood out starkly. He looked hopeless. He shrugged and then stood up, pushing back the chair. "I'll get out of your way for now."

"You don't have to leave. We can talk while we wait for them if you want."

He froze, looking like he wanted to sit back down with me but also like he was afraid to. "Um, I'm not sure it's a good idea right now."

"Let me guess? Part of you wants to sit here and talk, so you can stay close by me, but there's an independent part of your brain that's begging you to get as far away from me as fast you can."

He swallowed and a muscle in his cheek began to twitch. Something in the air between us changed and I could almost feel his fear, his tension, creeping into my own muscles.

"How would you know that's how I'm feeling? Can you read my mind now?"

I shook my head, relaxing back in the chair and trying to appear as harmless as possible. "I'm not able to read your mind or anyone else's. But I know what it's like to feel torn between two things. It's scary and uncomfortable. Makes you question everything, about yourself and life in general."

He let out a small breath of air and some of the strain eased from his shoulders, but he still didn't sit back down. His attention turned back to the windows, looking away toward something I couldn't see. For a moment, he looked young, unsure and the five years that separated us disappeared. "I feel like I need to be out there, trying to find the man killing those women. Stop him before it happens again. But I can't leave. Something inside won't let me. It makes me..." He didn't finish, his fists clenching as he fought with himself.

"Those situations make me angry." I said the words softly, hoping they would be of some comfort. "I like to be in control and when I feel like I'm not, well, it scares me. A lot. The way I usually react to being scared is to get angry. I did everything I could when I moved out here to build a life that I was in total control of. That way, I would feel safe and be sure that everyone else was safe from me."

"But you left this house and went to Angel Falls to stop that killer."

"Yeah, I did. But, if you look at how I did it, I made sure I was in control of everything from start to finish. I had a plan, which I planned and revised over and over until I felt like I had accounted for every possible eventuality. I did everything I could to make sure nothing would go wrong."

"And it worked."

I looked up, surprised to see he'd settled back into his seat, his hands on the table near mine. "I don't know if it worked out exactly as I envisioned," I said, "but it got the job done and I made it home. For example, I never dreamed that someone would think about following the paycheck or if they did, that it would ever lead them to me. Smart thinking on your part."

He smiled down at the table top, but in a brave movement, looked at me and met my eyes. The blue was stormy today, swirled with gray. They still looked pained, but maybe some of that had lessened since we'd started this conversation.

"I can't say it was smart, really," he said. "I just knew something felt off about the way you left. How you managed to take that guy out. It was too clean. He had the upper hand, he was bigger than you, but you still managed to walk away with only cuts and bruises. It was ..." He stopped and coughed, sounding almost embarrassed. "Well, it just seemed amazing to me."

"I don't recommend trying to take down a demon all by yourself, you know," I said, trying to keep my voice light. "Angus made sure I had training in case I ever needed to defend myself against an attack. Instead of using it as a defense, I turned it into offense. Not so hard when you know what you're doing. And Uncle Newt is a hard teacher. I'd been knocked around by him often enough that I learned a lot before ever thinking about taking on that Chaos Demon."

"See, that's what's going to get me." There was still a thread of disbelief running through his words. "The idea that there are all these different types of demons running around out there and I only know about two of them right now. The Chaos one and the creature that got into your house."

"The Proles," I offered.

He nodded. "Yeah, that one. But I saw pictures of the guy you killed, and he looked nothing like that other thing. How can they both be the same? And how will I know what they are before it's too late?"

I thought of how best to explain this to him. "Well, all demons were born from one source. But there are different types of demons, families you could say, each classified by what they do best. And they don't all look alike. Some have a more human form than others. Or can at least project one so they are more likely to blend in."

Torren was pensive, nodding his head as he followed along. "Like the one you called a Chaos Demon. He was good at causing chaos. The fight that started in the club when he was trying to lure the dancer outside away from everyone."

"Exactly. And the Proles is a child's demon. They like to

lead children away until they have them alone, and then they eat them."

He blanched at that and I couldn't disagree with him. It made my stomach hurt just thinking about it. No one had ever given me an idea of how many children had been stolen by Proles demons, but to me, even one was too many.

"What about the other ones you hear about in stories? Like a Succubus."

"They're out there." I gave him a wink. "So I've been told, at least."

His lips parted to ask me another question, but we were interrupted by the back door opening as Callum and Moose came back inside.

"You ready to go?" asked Cal.

"Sure. We were just waiting on you guys to finish up. I'll grab my stuff and we'll head over to the garage."

I picked up my purse, wallet, and the keys I needed for my SUV. With four of us and Torren's luggage, we'd need the space. Even if I had Moose shrink down to his smaller size, it felt like the guys took up a lot of space. Making sure they weren't sitting on top of each other could only improve our situation.

Chapter Twenty·Six

WITH ME LEADING the way out of the house, we all stepped into the backyard and headed toward the garage. As soon as we stepped outside the heaviest set of wards, the prickle over my skin told me we were moving beyond its protections. I let the guys go on ahead and turned back to face my home. I held my hands out, palms up, and whispered, "Protect," loading as much intent as I could into the word, asking the wards to please renew themselves and continue guarding my home while we were gone. I'd been taught that it never cost you anything to be polite, and even though there were practitioners that treated magic rudely, I'd never been that way. It always felt natural for me to ask for help from the stones.

I let the energy I held charged within me linger on my palms, until anyone with magical sight would have seen small flames leap to life, dancing on my skin. I whispered the word again, then pushed the flames out and away from me, directing it along the line of ward stones encircling the dwelling. The magic raced away from me, and I saw a haze of heat move around the house, following the lines I'd created, until they crossed each other, once, twice. As I stepped back, I heard the gentle hum as the wards recharged and swelled with the new energy I'd infused them with. It was a sound that always made me feel safe.

Catching up with everyone at the garage, I unlocked the SUV and we piled in. I appreciated that neither Cal nor Torren tried to take the driver's seat. This was my car, after all, and I was the one who drove it. It was time to hit the road.

I drove faster than I probably should have. I would have turned the radio on, but once we were on our way, Torren spoke up, peppering me with questions.

"So, about those demons again," he started.

I saw Cal look over at me and glanced back at him, meeting his eyes for a second before returning my attention to the road ahead. I answered his unspoken question. "Torren was asking about demons. It makes sense that if he's going to be stuck with us, he should have as much information as possible."

Cal didn't say anything, but out of the corner of my eye I saw his shoulders relax, dropping down a fraction.

Torren continued. It was obvious once he was interested in something, he didn't let up until his curiosity was satisfied. "You said demons all came from the same source.

So, what is it? Where do they come from?"

I swallowed, unsure what his response to the answer would be. Before I could say anything, Cal stepped in. "Angus is the source. He created them. Every single demon carries a kindred magic, one of his abilities. They're born with it."

"Like Delaney?"

Cal shook his head, shooting me a look that felt heavy as it settled on me. "Not in any way. She's the only one of her kind."

I blushed, surprised by my reaction to those words. Hoping to deflect some of the attention and lighten the serious atmosphere that filled the interior of the SUV, I said, "Torren, what do you know about Sirens?" I watched him in the rearview mirror and saw the shock on his face.

"Sirens are real? They're demons?"

"Yep. Angus made them too. Did you wonder why he chose to be a musician when he came Above?"

"Well, no, not really. I guess it just made sense. You know, the whole sex, drugs and rock n' roll thing."

I laughed. The fact that most musicians had a reputation for living wild lives had only given Angus even better cover when crazy things happened around him. "Sure, there's that. But Angus can use his voice to ensnare people. It's almost like when he sings he's casting spells on everyone listening. Compelling them to do what he wants them to do. Sirens inherited that trait from him."

Silence from behind me. I definitely had his attention. "Have you ever been to a concert where it just feels like there's this connection between the performer and the audience? Almost like you can feel the energy on the air?"

"Yeah, I guess. When the singer is really good."

"What you feel on those occasions is real especially if the singer is someone like Angus."

"Or you." This was Cal's quiet contribution to the conversation. I would have kicked him right then if I could.

"Wait, what? You can do that too?" Torren asked, his voice hesitant now. I had been trying to alleviate some of his fear around me, and it felt like I'd been making progress. Two steps forward, one step back. As Angus would say, we all end up in Hell either way.

I sighed. "Yes, Torren, I can do that too." I felt my next words deserved special emphasis. "If I want to. Which is why I don't sing around anyone anymore. It's too easy to lose myself to the music and I don't want to spell anyone by mistake."

"Another reason you live way out here?" he asked.

"Exactly. I even work from home. It keeps me from endangering other people." I swallowed against the guilt lodged in my throat, purposely not mentioning my call to his office or the information I'd gotten from Tausha.

This seemed to reassure him. He leaned back against the seat, his eyes looking out the window before they met mine in the mirror. He had a lopsided grin on his face and he seemed relieved. "So, tell me more about the Succubus."

Callum laughed in the front seat beside me and I joined in. I let Cal take over the history lesson and concentrated on getting us all to town in one piece.

Rolling into Hazelwood, I realized this was the first time I'd come into town this many times in such a short period. My last visit was the only time I hadn't arrived alone. Now, not only was I not alone, but I had another man with me and we were going to be moving his luggage out of the hotel and into my vehicle. People were going to notice.

The red brick of the Hazelwood Bed & Breakfast towered up above us, the turrets reminding me of my favorite fairy tales. The front rose up almost three stories and the black slate of the roof glistened when the sun hit it. Walking up the wide front stairs, I let my hand glide along the cold wrought iron railing, loving the intricate design built into this practical piece. Always well kept and welcoming, it was no surprise business was thriving for Donna Kay. The fact that she had a full salon always working for her in the back only added to her success.

When we entered the front doors, Donna Kay swept toward our little group. Even Moose, in his Yorkie form and decked out in his purple leash, benefited from the kind smile of the owner. Her short honey brown hair was perfectly done with no hint of gray, making it hard to place her age. Judging by the look in her keen eyes, she was dying to pull me aside and get the story behind my entourage.

"Delaney," she said, reaching out to grab my hands but then stopping herself with visible effort. She was a hugger. It made me appreciate her restraint even more. "It's so good to see you. You almost never come to town and now it's twice in two weeks. When will I get to work on your gorgeous hair? I can see you're letting it grow, but we could find time to clean it up for you."

All during this, she was guiding us toward the front desk, where one of her new employees was laying out paperwork for signatures and a bill to be paid. The guys followed behind us, Cal still managing to look distractingly masculine even as he held the sparkly leash attached to Moose. We were a sight, I'm sure.

"Mr. Bishop, we just have a couple things for you to sign and then I've got some people ready to help you with your things. I take it you'll be staying out at Delaney's place?" Damn, the woman should be a private investigator with her nose for news and her willingness to dig until she found answers. I think it was only her bone deep kindness that kept her from unleashing that skill on the world.

Torren signed the bill and we made sure everything was paid up. Donna Kay kept talking, her gentle voice a calming bit of background noise, until it was time to get Torren's luggage loaded. She fluttered her hand toward the grand staircase, giving Torren and Callum a pointed look. "I've got my nephew up there waiting to help you bring down the luggage. Go on up with your key and he'll help you bring everything down. Please make sure you call him James. He gets real stubborn if you try to call him Jimmy or anything like that."

Cal and Torren looked dazedly at her and I had to wonder if this was Donna Kay's magic power. Her conversation drew you in with little bits of information, but the whole time she was observing and assessing. Fluttering her hands, she got the men moving up the stairs, Moose being transferred over to an excited young girl whose sole job was to take care of the puppy guests. She pulled Moose out to the back yard for a little walk, and just like that, I was left alone with Donna Kay.

"Well young lady, you look like you've been through the wash a few times lately." She led me toward the sitting room, windows letting in the streaming fall light. "Miss Tilly called right after I hung up with you. Said you needed reminding that she's waiting to meet your men. All of them, she said. She was very specific."

I didn't even question how Miss Tilly had known I was going to be in town or muster an ounce of surprise. I rested my head in one hand for a moment. I had forgotten. With everything else going on, it had simply slipped my mind.

"Since you're in town, there's no time like the present. I got the sense there was something pressing she wanted to talk with you about. And them. I've got those little cakes she likes, so I wrapped some up for you to take over to her after we're done here. A sort of peace offering, you know. I've found a little sugar always makes things better." She reached out to pat my hand, but stopped herself again, her fingers curling into a fist. Her energy was bright and constant, and I had to wonder if the woman ever slept. She was always like this, any time we encountered each other.

"Now, do you have everything you need to take care of your guests? I know Ernie would be happy to deliver things out there from the grocery store but, if he's not available, you can always call here and I'll have James pick it up and bring it on out to you."

"I think we'll manage. I don't want to trouble any of you."

"No trouble at all sweetie. We take care of each other around here. You know that." Her words warmed me, filling a small hole inside that I hadn't realized was empty.

"If you know of anyone in town who has a bed I could buy, that would save me a trip to Omaha. I've got a small room I've been using for storage, but we're going to move things around so Torren's not stuck sleeping on the couch."

"Oh, so you're using all the bedrooms out there then," Donna said, her voice betraying no hint of curiosity. I'd seen the light in her eyes before she'd turned her head, so I knew she'd been wondering if one of the men was sharing a room with me.

"Yep. We're a full house now. I feel bad that Torren's going to be in such a small room, but it's better than not having a bed at all."

She laughed softly and nodded. "Course it is. It just so happens that I have a spare bed that I've never needed to use. I was going to set up a small single in one of the back turret rooms but ended up using it as my closet. So many shoes and purses I don't know when I'll ever use them all. The bed frame and the mattress have been in the storage room the last year or so. Never been used. The mattress is still wrapped up in the plastic."

"Oh, Donna Kay. Thank you." I tried not to gush but it was such a relief to have this small worry solved for me. "How much do you want for it?"

"How about one-fifty?" she asked. "That way, I feel like I'm getting something for it and you feel like I'm not just giving it to you. We're both happy."

"Okay, if you're really sure that's enough."

"Absolutely. It'll be nice to have space in that storage room again too. I'll have James bring it out to your house later on. That should give you plenty of time to visit with Miss Tilly and take care of that."

I sighed. Something told me that conversation wasn't going to be an easy one. But it had to be done.

"Thank you. I really do appreciate it. I'll just give him the cash when he drops it off."

"Perfect. And I'll make sure he knows to help carry it in and set it up. Full service." Her attention turned to the stairs behind me. "Oh good. Here come your young men. And your dog. Perfect timing."

We all filed out the front doors and down to the SUV. Torren had more things than I'd expected him to have. We managed to fit everything into the rear cargo area without too much trouble, and I thanked Donna Kay again as we began piling into the vehicle.

"Don't you worry about it. Now, go take care of your business with Miss Tilly. James will be out to your house later on."

I nodded and waved goodbye, then climbed into the driver's seat. As I shut the door, Cal said, "What business with Miss Tilly is she talking about?"

I wanted to groan but suppressed it. "Miss Tilly wants to meet all three of you," I answered, looking back at Moose to make sure he understood he was included in this. "I guess there are things she wants to discuss with us."

Cal nodded, understanding, but Torren was clearly in the dark. "Who's Miss Tilly and why do we care if she wants to talk with us?"

I sighed. "Miss Tilly is a very important person. She knows things and sometimes, she shares that knowledge with the people who need it. Think of her as the matriarch of this entire town. Everyone here listens to what she says and she's very highly respected. Listen to what she says, and if she asks you a question, answer it. Honestly. If you try to lie, she'll know, so don't even bother."

His only response was a loud sigh as he leaned back in his seat. Buckling up, I started the car and headed straight to

Miss Tilly's. Somehow a wrapped plate of sweet cakes had found its way into the car with us and was sitting on the center console between the front seats. I hadn't seen anyone sneak those in but was glad they had. Hopefully, it would be exactly the peace offering I needed it to be.

CHAPTER TWENTY·SEVEN

WE WERE ALL silent on the short drive to The Hedgerow. As I parked, I tried to calm my frantic heart rate. Somehow, I knew what Miss Tilly had to tell us was not good news. I fought to corral my mind and keep it from wandering when it had no clue where to go, but it was hard. There was nothing else I could do but walk in and find out what she knew.

Anywhere else, most people would have wondered about the strange group we made. Two big men, a dog and me, walking into an herbal store that sold soaps and teas and any natural remedies you might need. But the people who lived in Hazelwood were different. This was just another day and we were just like everyone else, going to Miss Tilly when we needed help. Or when she called on us to show up.

Pulling open the door, the chimes rang as they always did but this time the heavy scent of crushed rose petals greeted me as well. I was surprised to see a law enforcement officer talking with Miss Tilly in the back of the store. A young woman with bright blonde hair approached me immediately, a warm smile on her face.

"Hello, I'm Aften, Miss Tilly's granddaughter. She's busy with someone right now. Is there something I can help you find?"

"Sorry, but no. Thank you though. We were at Donna Kay's and she said Miss Tilly asked us to stop by. We'll come back later. It's no problem."

She put a hand out. "No, I think you should stay. You're Delaney, aren't you?"

I glanced up at her, surprised by the foggy sound of her voice and saw that her eyes were unfocused. It was just for a moment, then they cleared, and her gaze was bright and direct again. "That's right. I'm Laney. Do you want us to wait outside?"

Aften shook her head, glancing back at where her grandmother stood. "No, she's finishing up now. We've had lots of things to do. Storm's a 'coming." The way she said that made me think she'd heard it a lot lately, probably from Miss Tilly herself.

I could see the officer was making her goodbyes. Miss Tilly walked with her to where we were clustered, the men standing carefully, trying not to knock anything over. Moose seemed to be the most comfortable of all of us, sitting on the cool wood floor, his tongue out in a friendly way.

"Girl," said Miss Tilly, as she reached us. "It's about time. You made me remind you, but you're here now. So, we forgive and forget."

"Ms. Murphy?" asked the officer.

I studied the woman standing in front of me, carrying the weight of her uniform and gear with an easy grace that impressed me. Her thick black hair was pulled into a twist at the back and her mocha skin glowed even in the store's dim light. She was striking, an obvious strength running through her you couldn't miss.

"Yes. It's nice to meet you."

With a kind smile, she said, "I'm Lana. Lana Kingston. Nice to meet you as well."

"Oh, I recognize your name. You're the Washington County Sheriff, aren't you? I'm sorry. We didn't mean to interrupt."

"Oh no, I'm pretty sure Miss Tilly was done with me. She knew you were coming by and we just had a few things to discuss." Turning away from me slightly, she nodded respectfully to the older woman. "Thank you again for the information, Miss Tilly. I'll make sure my deputies know what to watch for." Her attention on me again, she said, "And Ms. Murphy. If you need anything out at your property, don't hesitate to call. I can have a deputy swing by anytime."

I smiled a thank you, then waited as she left the store before taking a deep breath and returning my focus to the reason we'd come here. "These cakes are for you Miss Tilly. Donna Kay told us they're your favorites."

The old lady grinned and clapped her hands like a young girl. "Oh, that one. She knows the way to ease things for everyone. She's buttering me up." She winked at me. "And it's working. Aften, some plates please."

We followed Miss Tilly over to the corner I'd joined her in the last time we'd talked. She had some small chairs pulled up to accompany the two upholstered ones that normally sat there. She'd obviously been expecting us. Holding her hands out, she said, "Everyone sit. No time to waste on being polite so we'll have to eat while we plan."

As we all took a seat, Miss Tilly pointing me to the upholstered chair next to hers, I had the distinct feeling I wouldn't like what was coming. If she was taking it so seriously that we couldn't sip some tea and discuss it in what she considered to be a civilized manner, we were in trouble.

Aften brought plates and began serving up the small cakes, passing them around to everyone. She then stood behind her grandmother's chair, clearly planning to listen in on everything we said.

Miss Tilly saw me notice Aften behind her and reached up to grasp her granddaughter's hand. "Aften is learning the Way now. She'll be taking over for me when it's time." She let her steely gaze rest on each of us, before continuing. "Now, there is evil coming here. I've felt it for a while, but it's close and we have taken steps to protect our town.

Aften and I blessed the Stones that surround this place, so evil will not be able to enter. But outside of town, where you live, Girl, that will fall outside the circle. You've set your Stones?"

I nodded. "I have. Recharged them before we left to come here. Cal and Moose checked for any weak spots as well. That's really just for the house. We have some smaller protections around the fence line and the garage, but there's too much land to try to circle right now."

She agreed with me. "Yes, the Stones we have were set long ago and built up over time. Even when I lived in your house, there was no need to weave the spells around all the acres."

"Why was the Sheriff here?" Cal asked.

"Oh, I told her what to prepare for. She needs to be on guard, and so does everyone she works with. She will lead, they will follow."

Torren's voice was coated with disbelief. "The Sheriff believed it when you told her that something bad was on its way and is mustering the troops?"

I tried to warn him with my eyes, knowing that his tone would not sit well with Miss Tilly. And it didn't.

"You are being rude, Boy. I don't allow rudeness here. That is your warning, the only one I will give. Now, be quiet and listen." Her voice was cold, her back straight and her eyes not leaving his. "This is my place and you will offer respect."

She turned back to the rest of us and I swear I heard a small sigh of relief from Aften that matched mine. I'd tried to tell Torren that Miss Tilly was not to be trifled with, but some people have to learn things on their own.

"The Stones are strong and will prevent this evil from entering our town. But you have to be prepared to face what comes." She turned her head to focus on me. "I have seen this is coming for you, Girl, filled with hate and anger. It knows you."

I didn't have an answer to that. Whatever was coming, how it knew me, I didn't understand yet, but I would do all I could to face it.

"We will warn our people and they will be watching. If they see anything, we will spread the word."

I started to ask a question, but she held her hand up sternly, silencing me. Her focus was locked on Callum, intensely surveying him before she spoke.

"You are a warrior, that is easily seen. There is more within you, but it's cloudy." She waved her hands quickly, as if trying to clear the air before her, but then shook her head in disappointment. "You've saved her once already, but I feel you won't be able to save her in the end. She must make that choice for herself."

Her gaze shifted to Torren, now obediently silent. "You came here for your own reasons, now you're stuck. And you haven't been honest. The shadows don't hide your heart as they do his," she said, inclining her head back toward Cal. "Your intentions are good, but they can easily go wrong. Be careful."

Hearing this made me think of Angus and his fondness for reminding me of where all my good intentions were likely to end up.

Miss Tilly's voice continuing brought my focus back to her. "Aften, tell me what you see when you look at this Companion."

Her granddaughter did as she was ordered, stepping toward Moose and kneeling down to the clean-swept wood floor, resting her hand gently on his head. He stayed still, no hint of a reaction. She froze, silently evaluating my Hound, until easing her way carefully back, inch by inch, until she was at what might have seemed a safe distance. Standing, her voice hesitant, she said, "That's no ordinary dog."

Miss Tilly cackled, shivering the air around us. "Indeed. He's not ordinary at all. But he loves the Girl and will do whatever is required to protect her. Perhaps not so good at following her orders, but he may still learn." She lowered her head in a respectful nod. "A Hell Hound has never found its way into my store before. You are welcome."

Moose stood up in response, walking over until he was directly in front of her and sitting down at her feet, lifting his right front paw to her knee. His movements were controlled and obviously intentional, conveying a sense of gravity and appreciation for her kindness. She smiled at him, touched his paw in acceptance and then released it. He returned to sit at attention next to me.

"Time is up. Things we all must do now," she said, standing up. Her eyes seemed to peer into the far away for a second before focusing on what was directly in front of her. "I believe someone is waiting for you at the house. Or will be. It's important. Goodbye."

Dismissing us, she stepped aside to let us file past. As I was about to follow everyone out of the store, she stopped me, her deft fingers quickly sneaking a small vial into my palm. "The things I sent with you before. You must add this to it when brewing. Your guardians will need it so you can do what must be done. Adding everything to cold water when it's ready is best. They won't taste it."

My mouth open in confusion, I was tempted to ask what she was talking about and how I would know when to use what she'd given me. A furtive shake of the head from Aften made me shut my mouth. Apparently, Miss Tilly believed things would become clear when necessary. I'd have to figure out the answers myself. She was only pointing me in the right direction.

I gave her my thanks and waved goodbye to Aften as she flipped the sign on the door to *Closed*, the lock clicking tight behind me. I could see through the front window that they stood together at the counter, silver and gold heads bent as they pored over something in front of them. The air around them looked hazy, and I wondered if it was the glass or a glimpse of the magic weaving between them.

Joining my entourage in the car, we sat in silence for a moment, processing the things we'd been told. There were a lot of holes that we needed information to fill in. It was reassuring to know that no matter what happened in the coming days, Hazelwood was protected, but that protection could only extend so far.

As we drove out of town, I decided to stop at the markers to examine them, test their energies and compare them to my own. The gleaming black stones appeared ornamental to those who didn't know better. But I'd recognized the hum they generated the very first time I'd come to Hazelwood. It had been an instantaneous sign that this was where I needed to be. Someone had planted flowers around the monument that welcomed visitors to the town, native wildflowers that were often used in natural healing remedies. The people here had planted their beliefs where anyone could see them, but I was just as sure that most people weren't able to read the signs.

My car pulled safely off to the side, I got out and approached the slabs of hematite shining in front of me. Even in the car, I'd felt the vibrations coming off them and getting closer, my teeth began to ache as the waves of energy got stronger. One stood tall enough that I could rest my hands down on top of it without sinking to my knees. I waited, my senses falling down into the depths, seeking out the magic that powered them.

It took a few seconds, but when I felt the zing through

my fingertips, I knew I'd found what I'd been looking for. This magic was ages old, probably set by the very first settlers of this little town. The scent of crushed roses floated up around me, similar to what I smelled in Miss Tilly's store, and what Aften had smelled like when she first greeted me. Not only was this magic old, I was sure it had been established by Miss Tilly's ancestors. The spell itself was similar to the one I'd used with my stones, but supported by a deep foundation, magic built layer upon layer, reinforcing itself year after year. There was safety in the stones, but goodwill also, and it explained how Hazelwood had stayed so prosperous. I recognized the welcoming feeling I'd encountered when I'd first come to this town and understood now why I'd immediately wanted to stay. These spells were strong and made to last. I was confident the town was safe. It was time to head home and get to work.

CHAPTER TWENTY EIGHT

PULLING INTO the drive, I was surprised to see a truck waiting, but then remembered Donna Kay's promise to send out a bed. The frame stood up in the back, the mattress resting against it. The young man who got out of the driver's seat waved his hand in greeting. I recognized the person in the passenger seat as soon as he opened the door. Ernie had come along as an extra pair of hands, though I suspected he really wanted to check in on my dog.

Sure enough, when we stepped out of the SUV, his eyes shone as soon as he spotted Moose walking along beside me on his leash. Clapping his hands and walking toward us, he called out, "Oh wow, you did keep him. I was hoping you would."

He crouched down, reaching out his hand to Moose for examination, then scratching his ears when Moose offered them up. "Seems like he's doing okay out here. And his paw is all healed up."

"He's doing really well. I feel like I've been adopted," I said, teasing him. But it was true. I did feel like Moose considered me family, regardless of why he'd been sent here in the first place.

Ernie smiled up at me, then stood. "Guess we better get this unloaded and into the house for you. Donna Kay was pretty specific." He copied her voice perfectly, saying, "Get it all inside and set up. No stealing cookies or wasting time. They have serious things to do out there and can't spend precious minutes babysitting you boys." He laughed and turned back to his friend. "Let's go, Man. I don't wanna miss out on that dinner your aunt promised us."

I opened the door for them as they lifted the bed frame up and began staggering toward the house. Cal and Torren were lugging in the box spring behind them and I whispered the words that would allow them to pass back and forth without a worry. With the four guys working together, the bed was easily set up in the small bedroom upstairs, and I sent the boys on their way with extra cash in their pockets and an envelope filled with the agreed amount for Donna Kay.

Torren began carrying his belongings upstairs, Callum behind him with a couple bags in each hand. I took that moment to slide into the kitchen and hide the little vial from Miss Tilly among my stash of herbal teas. If I needed to get to it, hopefully no one would pay any attention and assume I was making tea yet again.

I rested against the counter top, my thoughts whirling.

The need to do anything bubbled inside me, itching under my skin. I was restless, a feeling I hated because I knew it meant I was scared. The heavy sounds of furniture moving around upstairs provided some distraction, but not enough. I chewed at the skin along the side of my nail as I tried to sort out who could want to hurt me so badly that they would kill women who resembled me even slightly. But I couldn't think of any connections.

Steps on the stairs drew my attention away from my thoughts and I looked up, surprised to see Cal. "Already done up there?"

He shook his head. "Big stuff is taken care of. Torren's putting the last of his things away. I need to meet with Angus."

"Really? Why?"

"He calls, I answer. That's all I know, Laney."

"When are you supposed to meet with him?"

"Right now." His eyes drifted behind me, and I turned to see my father standing in the backyard. He was tapping his foot, like Cal was keeping him waiting.

"Okay, let's go see what he wants."

"No. Just me. He was specific about that."

I was shocked, speechless as he walked by me and out to where Angus waited.

Through the kitchen window, I watched Angus and Cal, their heads bent close as they discussed things my father didn't want me to hear. Moose rested in his bed in the corner, seemingly uncaring about my curiosity as I worried over the different things they might be talking about. It was an intent conversation if Cal's rigid posture was any indication, but I really had no idea what it could be. Chewing my lip in frustration, I finally pushed open the back door and stepped out.

Seeing me, Angus nodded to Cal, handed him a small box that might have been made of wood, then clasped him on the shoulder before walking toward me.

I gave my father what I hoped was a charming smile. "Seems like you two had a lot to talk about. Care to share?"

Angus shrugged. "There were things he needed to be aware of. I don't have a lot of time right now and I know Callum isn't going to pester me with countless questions."

"Hey, you've always told me information is the most important currency. Don't be mad that I listened to you."

He let out a brief laugh, then sobered up quickly. "Delaney, I love you. More than I can ever explain. I've taken steps to keep you safe when I can't be here. Callum will tell you more. Please listen to him." Kissing my forehead, he walked away, vanishing when he reached the trees, far enough away that I didn't feel even a hint of the pressure from his departure.

I turned away from where my father had gone, to face Cal. "Let me see what he gave you."

"Once we're inside Laney. We need to make sure we're not overheard."

"You stood out here with Angus and didn't worry about that. Tell me what's going on."

Cal's jaw was set, his next words sharp. "Your father and I were surrounded by a silence spell, which he set so no one would hear what we were saying. Besides, what he told me pertains to everyone."

I let Cal lead me back into the house. Patience had never been one of my virtues, but if this was truly that important and Torren needed to know about it, I could wait a few minutes. I just wished my father had come right to me with it.

When we walked into the kitchen together, Torren was waiting for us. "So, what was that all about?"

Cal set the box my father had given him on the table in front of me, gesturing at me to open it. Shaped into a pentagon, the wood had been intricately carved with wings spilling out from a central point. It was truly beautiful work. Laying my hand on the top, I felt power radiating from within and opened the cover. Nestled on soft blue velvet were four pieces of leather. I lifted the largest one, gasping as I saw the design cut into it. Thorns had been tooled across the front of it, small crystal roses a red accent at random intervals. Cal reached for it and gently wrapped it over the sensitive scars on my left wrist, covering the bright ridges from view.

"Your father was concerned the scars left by the Proles would make it easy to identify you. He had this commissioned for you." I sucked in air as I felt the magic running through the butter-soft leather. It tickled at my skin before settling to a comfortable hum.

"What are the other things in there?" asked Torren.

Cal lifted the remaining pieces out and handed one to him. "These are for us to wear, all the time."

I looked up sharply at that, some of my joy dimmed by this announcement and suspicious of my father's motives. "Why is it so important that you always have them on?"

He met my gaze without flinching. "All of us need to wear these, including you. Your father had protections built into these for each of us. They'll also allow us to find each other if we need to."

"Trackers?"

"They're more than that, Laney." I could tell that Cal was trying to keep his tone soothing, but that only needled me more. "There were protection spells layered into the leather as it was prepared. Each red stone set in there can be charged with energy so you're less likely to need to draw on one of us in an emergency. Angus knows how much you want to avoid that."

That was at least considerate. "But you'll all be able to find me wherever I go?"

"If we are separated or something happens, the cuffs will help us locate each other. That's all. These are not meant to be anything other than a back-up system in case things go wrong."

I nodded, a tightness in my chest taking me by surprise. My father had thought of me when planning this but he'd also considered Callum, Torren, and Moose. He'd recognized their safety was important to me. Cal knelt down next to my dog and took off the sparkly purple collar he'd been saddled with wearing since he'd come into my house.

"This is for you, Hound. Wear it well. It will change with you as needed."

Moose licked Cal's hand as a thank you, then settled back down, his paws crossed in front of him, the very picture of sincere canine repose.

Torren held up the strip of leather that Cal had set in front of him, his jaw set. "I don't wear jewelry."

"It's not jewelry. It's a tool to keep us all safe."

"Are you going to wear that one all the time?"

Cal took what I assumed was a calming breath. "Yes. I'm going to wear it all the time. Because doing that means I'm more prepared to keep Laney safe."

I held out my hand for the cuff Torren was examining. "May I see it?"

He handed the leather to me and I turned it to decipher the design. "This is really amazing work," I whispered, awed. Stars repeated across the surface, dye worked into the edges of the stars until they almost glowed. I handed it back to Torren, then grabbed Cal's. A series of swords and shields did battle, telling a story about him I didn't have enough information yet to fully decipher. Warrior. That much I understood. "Well, it's obvious Angus put some very specific thought into each one of these."

"He did." Cal leaned toward me from across the table. "We should be able to use them to transmit some spells if we have to, as well. If one of us is hurt or in danger, you might be able to channel your shield spell to one of us for a bit."

"That could come in handy." My voice was higher than normal, words coming quickly in my excitement at the idea. "I hope it gives us enough time to get there and deliver help in person."

"Your father will be glad you appreciate his gift."

"He's not a bad guy, most of the time. Overbearing, yes. Overprotective, absolutely. But not bad. Not around me, at least."

Cal seemed to find that funny, but he never explained exactly why.

CHAPTER TWENTY·NINE

WITH THE ADDITION of Torren to the house, our routine had to change again. Being close to me eased something in him, his angry tension gradually fading. We found a balance somehow. Callum started working one on one with Torren, teaching him some of the history of magic while explaining demons. They went over the different types, what their skills were. Most importantly, what their weaknesses were.

Cal also found excuses to get Torren out of the house from time to time. They were nearby, tinkering in the garage or keeping up with the maintenance things I took care of before. It gave me room to breathe, and it helped Torren test his limits when he was away from me.

This morning, Cal had mentioned seeing marks around one of the ward stones guarding the house. It looked as if someone or something had tried to dig it up. The two of them struck out for the back edge of my land, looking for any other signs that danger was nearby. Moose was given the task of staying with me, making sure I was safe inside. I watched them walk away and turned to the notes I had strewn across my desk. I needed to refresh my own memory of demonology. Uncle Newt had drilled me on this information, focusing on each demon's weapon of choice, from magical strengths to pure brawn. My earlier education had been brief and really only hit the highlights, prepping me for which demons were most likely to think I tasted good and where to hit them so they'd change their minds. Those had been my lessons when I'd first moved out here, but since little had threatened, I hadn't kept up the knowledge. Now I needed it. Fast.

Moose launched up from his position at my feet, a low growl vibrating from his throat. He paced the floor next to my desk, walking a circuit along the front windows, then back to me, only to do it all over again. Leaning over, I ran my fingers over the silky fur at the top of his head, scratching soothingly. He submitted to the attention for a moment before returning to his sentinel stalking, releasing more growls from time to time. His head was cocked to the side, like he was listening for something I couldn't hear.

I had a nagging feeling that something wasn't right, and there was no way that random demons were finding their way to me just because I'd killed one of their own. Both Angus and Newt had reassured me that my resonance hadn't changed and there wasn't a demon attracting beacon flashing overhead. So why had the Proles been sent here? As my thoughts wandered, turning over possible connections, I found myself wondering about the man Torren had seen that day in the coffee shop? Was he involved in this somehow? Did he even exist?

I huffed out a breath in disgust with my inability to harness the thoughts swirling inside my head. I wasn't going to figure this out right now, but that didn't mean I couldn't do something productive. Like target practice. With knives.

Standing up and stretching, I rotated my neck, letting the muscles relax and ease the stress I was starting to feel gather in my shoulders. Just when I was ready to head to the basement to work on my aim, Moose let loose a howl and threw himself toward the back of the house, shifting from the sweet, small dog that had been pacing my floors to a large black streak as he ran. The back door crashed open as he hit it full force and I raced to keep up with him. Making it to the back porch stairs, I spotted two figures running toward me. There was a wave of movement behind them, hazy in the distance. My first thought was that the trees were just moving with the wind. But then my vision cleared, and I could make out the lumbering figure following behind them.

The bracelet on my wrist flared with sharp electricity, stinging me into action. I followed Moose down to meet Torren and Callum as they tried to make it back to the safety of the ward stones that would keep everything out as soon as they crossed the boundary. The magic was in place, the familiar hum in the back of my mind confirming it was strong, fully charged. I didn't leave them down at all any more, unwilling to risk another demon slipping in the way the Proles had. But I wanted no delays barring Cal and Torren from their path to safety. I connected with the stones, dropping the wards in readiness.

Both men were running full out, legs eating up patches of ground, but it was clear the creature was gaining on them. Moose stood in front of me at the edge of the stones, his muscles tense. He rested his long body against my legs, pushing me back, keeping himself between me and the coming danger. I rested my hand on the new collar around his neck, feeling the flames chased into the leather, and then raised myself up to my full height.

"We have to help them. Now," I said, my voice firm. He whined, looking up at me and then back to the men. With a growl, he finally made up his mind and shifted his weight off me. We stepped forward together, our feet moving until we were running as fast as I could to meet our friends and stand with them.

As we closed the distance, I could hear Torren screaming at me to go back. Cal shouted a word that was caught by the wind and blown away from me. A brilliant sword burst to life in his hand and he stopped running, turning to face the coming giant. He planted his feet firmly and waited, letting the gap between himself and danger shrink, allowing Torren to draw a few more feet closer to safety.

Again, there was a shock through my arm from the cuff around my wrist. I spared a quick glance at it and saw the garnets were flashing with rare light, burning from within. Torren was about fifty feet away from us now, legs moving desperately, but it was clear that his stamina was gone. The creature that was charging made a keening sound as it recognized its prey was close.

For a moment, the helplessness I felt overwhelmed me and I was choking, unable to suck in enough air or move my legs fast enough to reach him. My feet were cinder blocks dragging through mud and I knew I'd never make it in time. I forced myself to push that feeling down, focusing only on striding forward, reaching his side and standing there as his protection. Moose woofed to get my attention, and I nodded, waving my hand toward Torren, giving him permission to run ahead of me.

That was all he needed, his burst of speed amazing me. He flowed over the ground, effortless and pure enjoyment, even as he ran into battle. I was the awkward runner flailing along behind, but I kept on going, putting my feet to the ground and pumping my arms as hard as I could. I heard the cadence of my feet repeating over and over in my head. "*Get There, Get There, Get There.*"

It felt like forever, even though I knew it couldn't be. Moose had reached Torren and barreled past him. He slid to a stop, a second line of defense behind Callum, who was eerily still, flames chasing up the blade of his sword. He barely seemed to breathe, his eyes never leaving the earthy figure bearing down on him. Just as I was afraid that Cal would let himself be trampled to death, he shifted his weight slightly to the right, his feet dancing around the creature as his sword swept out and landed on the back of the creature's leg. With a scream, it fell forward and tried to catch itself, its weight shaking the ground as I reached Torren's side.

I was close enough now to see the face of this creature, a formless lump of a nose and anonymous mouth, lidless eyes that stared as it shook and tried to stand again. Cal pressed his advantage silently, circling around and striking at skin that reminded me of the layers of clay I sometimes found when I was planting. The creature struggled to stand, gaining a knee as Cal continued to mark it with his sword, wounds that opened but didn't bleed. A massive hand shot out, trying to catch Callum unprepared but he ducked under it and swung around, his sword catching at the wrist and slicing through. The hand fell into the dirt and flopped, shaking as the creature wailed above it. Cal kept charging in, raining down strokes but the crying just continued, rising to such a pitch that I wanted to cover my ears even as Torren and I stumbled backwards.

With a sickening scream, the creature reared up, chunks of it flopping onto the ground, quaking like the hand had. As it fell back, away from Cal's sword, it cracked down the middle. Like dripping candle wax, skin slid to the ground, quivering as it struggled to reform. The monstrous thing fell back, its heavy weight crashing down with an impact that almost knocked me off my feet. With a moan, it collapsed into itself, what nerves it had dancing for a moment, before it settled and finally stilled.

Callum circled it once more, looking for any sign that it might surge upward on the attack again, catching his breath while he watched it. I tried to examine it from where I stood but was too far away to see any distinguishing features. It was nothing now, reminding me of a lump of clay waiting to be made into something.

"What the Hell was that?" asked Torren, his voice breaking the tense silence surrounding us.

"A Golem." Cal spat the words. "Formed and sent here with one mission. To attack and destroy."

"A Golem?" I repeated, unsure. "I've never heard anything about them."

Callum wiped his now quiet sword on his pants, the Golem drippings leaving brown streaks on his jeans. Sweat dripped from him and he was taking long breaths, riding out the adrenaline rush. When the sword's surface gleamed clean, he bowed over the blade, making me think he was thanking it its service. The sword flashed like quicksilver before disappearing with a ringing note left behind on the air.

That done, Cal turned to me and shrugged. "I'd have to

say Newton left out a chunk of your education. It probably never occurred to him that someone would ever send a Golem after you. They're creatures born from clay, animated by magic, driven to accomplish a single purpose."

That sounded ominous and generally awful. Someone had sent this here to attack my home.

"Just like the Proles," I whispered to myself.

Cal heard me, nodding sharply in agreement. Torren stared at us, his eyes wild. I stepped between them, needing to see up close this enemy that had been formed solely to fight me. I knelt down at the edge of the melted mass, trying to discern any clear marks that could tell me who had sent this thing. The smell rising from it was loamy but there was an unpleasant tang, something that made me think of burnt gristle.

There were puddles of melted skin from where Cal's sword had swept through, and some of these still bubbled and popped, letting out more of the meaty odor. My stomach twisted, and I was about to turn away when I saw a dark brown scrap poking out from the center, the edge of it barely visible.

I reached out a finger to test it and heard Moose whine behind me. I looked at him with what I hoped was a reassuring smile, then turned back to my assessment. Trying to grip the end I could see, I gave a gentle tug, expecting the piece of what felt like leather to slide free. Instead, the whole mass in front of me began to shake. The puddles of skin quivered and the noxious odor increased suddenly, pouring out putrescent fumes.

Shocked, I fell back and scrambled away. Cal's hands wrapped themselves in the back of my shirt, dragging me to my feet gracelessly. I watched as the fallen Golem in front of us coalesced into smaller figures that shook themselves, each one identical to the first. As a group, they turned their staring eyes right to where I stood.

CHAPTER THIRTY

CAL MUTTERED a curse in a language I didn't know. What had once been a single, enormous threat now surged forward in multiples. Torren grabbed my hand, dragging me back and out of the way. Callum growled, a sound full of frustration, and pointed behind us. "Get inside the stones. Be ready to set those wards." I nodded at him, and started to head that way, but his next words stopped me. "Even if we aren't there, you set those wards and keep these things out." I skidded, trying to turn back to him but Torren pulled me along.

Moose and Callum faced the oncoming swarm, each individual piece smaller than the original, but the sheer number of them was overwhelming. Cal's sword was back in his hand and he fought with Moose like they were a team. The surge of creatures was relentless, but they beat the mass back as much as they could.

Desperately watching over my shoulder as I tried to run,

I saw Moose catch one of the creatures that was leaping forward, knocking it back into the dirt and wrapping his jaws around its neck. He clamped down and then shook the thing mercilessly, flipping it up into the air. When it came back down, the body was motionless.

I was about ten feet away from the stones when one of the creatures made it past Callum and beyond even Moose, who was tearing into two of the creatures he'd batted down. I cried a warning at Torren who dropped my hand and turned to face what was coming. He dove forward to snatch up a tree branch from the ground and then rose to confront the danger gaining on us. He took a swing at the creature's head, but it ducked under the club's path. The thing feinted in and then twisted around as Torren tried to counter the move, leaving his side open. The creature's fist swung in and connected with a shocking thump. The impact of the body blow left Torren staggering, his knees fighting to keep him upright for a few seconds. He crumpled to the ground, unable to support himself, a brief scream of pain echoing.

I felt the ache in my side where Torren had been struck, felt my breath start to seize up, but then shook myself out of the feeling. Rushing to his side and sliding to the ground, I grabbed the stick he'd wielded in his own defense and swung at the creature that was coming in for the kill as I regained my feet. It flinched back and tried to maneuver around me, but I pivoted, following it steadily. When it darted in again, I waited until I could smell the fetid odor of its skin before I brought the stick up, catching it under the chin and enjoying the sound of what I hoped were its teeth smacking together.

I couldn't help myself as I barked out a harsh laugh, enjoying the fear I saw crawl across the creature's face. I didn't waste time reveling in the adrenaline that was fueling this fight. I stalked toward it, never taking my eyes from it, keeping my body between it and Torren.

It crouched in front of me, unmoving as I approached. I looked for hints, anything that I could use to gauge where it would jump to. It didn't appear to breathe, so I couldn't predict when it would come at me by its breathing patterns. I remembered everything Newt had taught me to look for in battle and none of it was helpful in this fight. It was going to boil down to the basics. The first thing he'd ever told me during our battle lessons was, "Winning ugly is still winning. Because it means you lived." I'd do what I had to do to make sure we all came out of this as healthy as we could.

I copied the creature's posture, its stillness, waiting. My hand gripped the club I carried as tightly as I could. I let my breath out beat by beat, counting my heartbeats in my head. Deprived of my movement and the sound of my frightened breathing, the Golem in front of me cocked its head, much like I'd seen Moose do when he was puzzling something out. I ignored the sounds of fighting coming from Callum and Moose's position and kept my focus centered on the problem directly in front of me.

It seemed like an eternity, but the moment finally came when the Golem couldn't wait any more. I saw the minute flexing in its legs as it prepared to leap at me and tensed my muscles in readiness. Its forward momentum carried it right at my head and I waited until the last second before I tucked down into a roll, coming up right behind the thing that threatened my home and my friends. I couldn't contain the scream that tore out of me as I swung my club at the Golem's head, my rage powering the impact as I followed through, hearing my father's patient voice as he tried to teach me how to hit a baseball when I was younger. "Keep your eyes open, Laney. And swing all the way through the damn ball."

The satisfying crunch of contact filled my ears and something wet flew out from the Golem's head before the branch got stuck. Letting my anger charge all the energy around me, an image of the bright blue purifying fire I'd used back in Angel Falls appeared in my mind. I focused on that and let it build, then shoved the magic out through my hands and into the creature that wavered on unsteady feet before me. The bright blue flames raced down the wood, into the Golem and shards of light burst out through cracks that spread over its skin. It turned to face me, hands trying to grasp my arms, but then collapsed onto its knees. It was motionless for a second before an uncontrollable quaking took it over, the cracks spreading and light spearing through as the gaps widened. When the Golem's entire skin was webbed with lines, its face creased with what I thought must be pain. It raised both arms to the sky, almost glowing, and exploded, the light inside bursting its way out. Chunks of Golem flew, liquefied for a moment until the purifying fire burned it all away.

I spared a glance at Torren, who was trying to stand, his hand protecting his injured side. We seemed to be out of danger for a brief moment. My attention on Callum and Moose now, I could see they were tiring. There were fewer Golems attacking, but we had been outnumbered from the beginning. I stepped forward, the scars on my wrist flaring white hot. The heat from the purification spell I'd used began to build around me again, electricity flaring as the energy rushed to my silent call. The stones on the bracelet shone a deep blood red as I raised my hands and pointed toward the attackers. I didn't need words any longer for the magic to know my request, and, as I dropped my arms down, I felt the energy arrow away from me, engulfing the attackers. Protecting those who I claimed as mine.

I could see the purification spell as it worked its way into each and every individual Golem, diving inside and spreading to fill them. The cracks webbed out across their skin and the group began to collapse, one by one, losing their strength and ability to fight. Callum and Moose retreated back, watching as the light began to blaze out from inside each and every creature, almost blinding when it reached its peak. Callum waved his arm, calling out to me, his voice sharp and staccato. The bracelet on my wrist sparked. A shield engulfed me just as the Golems exploded. The force knocked us all backwards, throwing us roughly to the ground.

CHAPTER THIRTY·ONE

THE IMPACT knocked the breath from me. I made it to my knees, then gave myself a few seconds to regain my balance and adjust to the ringing in my ears. When I felt like I could open my eyes without losing what little food I'd managed to eat earlier, I gave it a try. Both Callum and Moose were bloody and covered in dirt, but they were very clearly alive. Relief hit me hard. I didn't fight the tears filling my eyes.

Moose limped over, letting me rest my weight on him as I climbed unsteadily to my feet. Callum met my eyes, then his gaze traveled over me until he was satisfied that I had no pressing injuries. He started toward me but the stricken look that crossed his face as he looked past me made my stomach twist.

Wondering, I turned and gasped. Torren's body was crumpled on the hard ground, twisted painfully. The force of the blast had thrown him back to where the stones were waiting. The protective ring we'd been trying to get to had caught him, the blood from his head staining the shine of the stone he'd hit. He didn't move, not even to breathe and I felt my knees start to go out from under me. I wavered on my feet, but Cal was there, bracing me with a strong arm. Together, we made our way to where Torren lay.

Moose joined us, a sad whine communicating his worry. I knelt down next to Torren, reaching out to touch him but pulling back in fear. I didn't know how to help him or if that was even possible. Cal joined me, taking my hand in his with a comforting squeeze, then placing it on Torren's chest. There I could feel the smallest of vibrations, reassuring but slight, stuttering between beats. I hated feeling useless, but I really had no idea what to do. Moving him could hurt him more than he already was. The simple fact that he never had to be in harm's way at all made me angry at the circumstances that had pushed him into the path of the danger stalking me right now.

Callum seemed to know the thoughts plaguing me. He leaned in, his solid presence offering me support and solace. Quietly, he said, "You can help him. Drop your shields and share some of your energy. It will give his body the time to heal his injuries."

I held back, reluctant to even attempt something I'd fought to avoid for so long. "You can heal him, like you did when I was hurt." I could hear the childish stubbornness in my voice but couldn't stop it. "Even Angus thinks you're the best at it."

I could feel him shaking his head. "Delaney, he needs *you*. I can't help him the way you can. The two of you have already established a connection. His body recognizes you. His energy knows yours and will welcome it. I don't have that with him. Anything I try to do may hurt him even more as his body fights against what it thinks is foreign."

If we were down to this as our only option, things were far worse than I'd thought they would ever be. Understanding my hesitation, Cal covered my hand with his, I couldn't fight the necessity before me. "Close your eyes," he whispered. "Find the link between the two of you, focus on it and then drop your shields so that connection can fully open."

No time for arguing, I did as he said. I closed my eyes, scanning the darkness for whatever it was that kept Torren tied to me. Anxiety clawed at my insides as I saw nothing in the darkness. Cal's calming voice stopped the panic from rising. "Breathe and relax. You can do this."

I fought the urge to pull away and nodded, forcing a deep breath in and out, over and over again. As my body relaxed with the rhythm of my breathing, I began to see a thread of light running from Torren into the center of my chest. It seemed to pulse with the beat of my heart, becoming more distinct the longer I watched it. It looked so real, like I could touch it if I tried. Not opening my eyes, I reached a hand toward where I thought it would be. My hand felt nothing, but the connection vibrated as my fingers brushed over it, the sensation spilling into me with little spirals of light pouring off. I heard Torren's body move on the ground in front of me in reaction, so it was a connection that truly ran both ways.

Cal's voice came again. "Now that you've found it, drop your shields and allow your energy to flow down that line."

He made it sound easy but when I tried to release them, they didn't come down. I imagined taking them down, like dismantling a wall brick by brick, but nothing shifted. Afraid to lose that link with Torren in my mind, I kept that image of the brightly glowing thread behind my eyes and resorted to the only other thing I could think of. I begged.

"Please, please let me help him." My voice cracked at the end, but whatever I'd said seemed to work. Cal's gasp told me that he could feel the release as my shields lowered and my connection to Torren glowed even brighter.

"Now, Laney. Just share yourself with him, let it run down that link into his body." Cal sounded sure this was the right thing to do, but I didn't have his confidence. Humming a tune to myself, I imagined the melody blending with the light in front of me and filling Torren up. Shocked, I felt the connection we shared vibrate again, more solidly this time, and Tor shifted once more, his legs kicking out. I tried to pour more energy into the connection, scared I was doing something wrong, but Callum's voice reached me.

"That's enough Laney. You can shut it down. It worked."

I pulled back, ending the song and relaxing back, my butt hitting the ground. Hands shaking, I looked at Callum, who gave me a quick, tired smile. "What song were you using?" he asked.

"Just something Angus used to sing around the house when I was little." I shrugged, startled by how tight my shoulders felt from that simple movement.

"Oh," he said. "Well, it was nice. And it was a good idea. I think he's well enough that we can move him now."

Together, we managed to get Torren in the house, undressed and into his bed. I couldn't miss seeing the bruises that had already appeared on his body but chose to focus on the fact that Cal was right. Torren did look better overall. I did my best to ignore the pull I felt between us anytime I got close to him, shelving it along with some other questions I had. Cal was focused on checking Torren for any internal injuries that required immediate attention. He didn't need to be distracted by my desire for answers.

CHAPTER THIRTY·TWO

WHEN I WAS certain that Torren was as comfortable as we could make him and there was nothing else I could do, I left Callum to his healing work and made my way to the basement. Bare fisted, I took out my anger on Bob and a couple of the heavy bags. I was a sweaty mess soon enough, my hair dripping into my eyes and making them sting. I took a break for a quick drink and to wipe my face clean. Ready for another round, I walked out to find Cal waiting for me.

"You didn't have to leave," he said.

I shook my head. "There wasn't anything I could have done to help you with him, and I don't like feeling useless. Down here, I'm out of the way. I can't hurt anyone."

"Except yourself." He looked pointedly at my knuckles, which were cracked and bleeding now.

"A little blood, sweat, and tears never hurt anyone." I

tried for the half-hearted joke, but it sounded more pained than I wanted it to. "Well, blood and sweat, at least."

Callum came over to me, a warm cloth in his hands. He gently laid it over the cuts I'd made, making them sting. He held on even when I tried to pull away, and I felt the tickling sensation that told me he was healing them with the barest of skin contact. "Please don't," I said. "They'll heal fine on their own."

He didn't look up at me, his gaze on my busted knuckles. "Do you enjoy punishing yourself? Is this a human thing?"

I pulled back, but he still didn't let go. His eyes lifted to mine and there was an unmistakable challenge in them.

"This isn't about punishing myself. Or anyone else." I didn't hold back on the anger, letting it fill my voice. "This is about my life. About what a mess it's become lately."

Cal didn't flinch. He didn't even react, beyond a slight brow raise. "A mess? I don't see a mess."

"Oh really? Is this what you think passes for normal in someone's life? Golems exploding and Proles hunting us down? People tied to me when they didn't want to be?"

Cal's eyes flashed, shining in the dim light for a moment before the flare passed. "Oh, I see. You're feeling sorry for yourself. I've read about this. In every romance novel Newton gave me the heroine has this moment. Let's get it over with."

That pissed me off and I didn't hold back. "Are you joking? I'm nothing like someone you've read about in any of your books. And I don't appreciate you trying to compare me to them. I have every right to be angry when people force themselves into my life, which was perfectly fine before they showed up."

He nodded. "Yep, heroine has her life disrupted, her plans for the future are altered and she resents it. Pretty much like everything I've read." His voice was hard and even, void of emotion.

I opened my mouth to respond but realized he was right. I really was feeling sorry for myself. Angus and Uncle Newt would be disappointed in me if they could see this. My anger left me, and I slumped, drained and unsteady.

"You're right." I leaned back against the wall, needing the support. "I hate to admit it, but Hells, you're right."

He didn't gloat, just joined me against the wall. "Good, I'm glad we got past that quickly. We've got things to prepare for and I need you focused on the problem in front of us."

"The problem being someone or something out there wants us dead."

He shook his head. "I don't think that someone gives a damn about us. I think they're after you. The rest of us are just in the way."

"Great. I'm going to get you killed"

"No, you're not. We're going to find out what we're up against, then we're going to find a solution."

"And if we can't find the answers?"

"Then you'll find I'm harder to kill than you think I am." He leaned into me, his shoulder bumping mine in a friendly way.

I snorted. "That really doesn't make me feel better."

"Well it should. I've been through a lot and I'm still standing. Don't count me out yet." His voice was confident and coaxing. I couldn't fight the grin I felt coming. If his plan had been to make me feel better, it had worked. A little, at least.

"How's Torren?" I asked. Might as well get to the first problem we had.

Callum stilled but answered my question. "He's okay. Stable for now. What you did out there gave him a fighting chance. We'll have to see how he does. I managed to do some surface healing, but nothing too intense. His body's defenses are on high alert right now. If I pushed too hard, they'd have focused on me instead of on fixing him."

That was as good as it was going to get for the moment. So, on to the next problem. "Can you explain something to me?"

"I guess that depends on what the question is. I'll do my best." Cal's voice was hesitant, but he said he'd try so I'd work with that.

"Torren was bound to me so easily. But, when I wanted to help him, it was hard for me to find the connection and know how to use it. Why?"

Callum pushed up away from the wall and turned to face me. "Binding can happen quickly or over time. It depends on the circumstances."

"Okay. Makes sense, I guess."

"Torren kissed you. Surprised you with it."

I nodded. "Yeah, so what? I know physical contact impacts a binding. That's why I've tried so hard to avoid it."

"It's not just physical contact, although that can spur the process along. Intentions matter. Desire matters."

"Are you saying that Torren wanted to be tied to me?"

Cal stopped me. "No. I'm saying he felt a need to protect you, and that he wanted to kiss you. Put those things together with some intense physical contact when your shields came down, and that was it. He was bound."

"But if it was that easy to bind him, why isn't it just as easy to release him?" I needed the answer to this question. If there was a way to release him as soon as he was healed, I desperately wanted to be able to do that for him.

"I told you, intentions matter. Both parties have to want the bond to be released. If they don't, it's a losing battle."

"But Torren wants to be free. He freaked out when we told him what happened. And I don't want to keep him here against his will. I've never wanted anyone to be stuck with me."

Cal sighed. "You know relationships are never that easy, Laney. Once you have that history with someone, it's hard to let go of them. It seems like there's always a little part of you that holds on. Remembers the good times. The good feelings. This is just like that, but on a deeper scale."

"I don't know, actually." I tried to keep my voice

controlled, but I could feel the hurt running underneath it. I was hoping he didn't pick up on it.

"What do you mean?" Cal asked, sounding genuinely confused.

"Relationships. Like you said. I don't really know anything about them or how they work."

"Wait a minute. What?"

"I've been on one date in my life. You've already heard how that ended."

"Delaney look at me." The command in his voice was obvious but he wasn't trying to coerce me. He was just serious. I met his eyes and stopped trying to hide my discomfort. The look on his face was intent, focused solely on me.

"You've never kissed someone without worrying about how they would be affected?" He was hesitant, almost like he was afraid he'd scare me off if he pressed too hard.

I shrugged. "Well, the first time, I didn't have any idea this could ever happen. After that, I tried to avoid physical contact with people in general. Angus is really the only guide I've had to this and even he doesn't always understand how his gifts work within me. So, trial and error is my only option, and I'm not willing to risk hurting someone. With all of that, avoidance worked pretty well."

"Until Torren." His calm understanding lifted a weight from me for a moment. "You've never had any intimate contact then. Beyond kissing."

An embarrassed heat flared through me, my skin

blushing with it. I stepped away from him, my hands curling into fists. "If simply kissing someone causes this much trouble, I hardly think sex is a good idea."

He grinned a little wickedly for a moment, like he was considering the idea, then his jaw returned to its serious set. "I think for you, the problem is that you've never had the chance to experience any of this without always worrying that it could hurt someone. Imagine what it would be like if you could. If you could let go and enjoy yourself the way anyone else would, without trying to protect everyone." The glint in his eyes turned mischievous. "Hells, you might find you really like it."

"Yeah, not going to happen. Apparently, I'm irresistible or something."

"Of that, I have no doubt." Callum stepped closer. "What did your father tell you about me?"

I narrowed my eyes at the question, which seemed out of place. "What do you mean? He said he sent you, that you were going to help protect me."

"Did he give you any reason for why he chose me to protect you? Instead of someone else?"

I really didn't understand where he was going with this. "He didn't elaborate. Just said there are some secrets he wasn't meant to tell. That when we had time, I should ask you directly."

"Did you ask him if there was any chance you could bind me?" He closed the distance between us a little more as I thought back to that conversation with Angus.

The lack of space between us was making it hard for me to breathe. I tried to back away but his hand on my arm stopped me. "Did you ask him about binding me?" he questioned me again, his voice stronger, more determined for an answer.

I cast around for the answer, trying to remember everything Angus had told me in that conversation. He'd refused to tell me what Callum was, where he came from or anything about his past. But when I pressed him, he had said there was only one way Cal could be bound to someone.

"Yes," I admitted. "I did ask him about that. Because if there was any possibility, I was going to ask him to send you away. I didn't want to screw you up too."

"And since I'm still here, I assume he told you that you won't be able to."

I nodded. "He said that could only happen if it was your choice."

A lazy smile slid over his face. "The Devil really is in the details, isn't it?"

Panic I didn't understand rose up inside me, my stomach flipping. "What are you talking about?"

"This is why Angus sent me here. Because you can't bind me. But I can bind myself, if I want to."

CHAPTER THIRTY·THREE

HIS FINGERS still on my arm, he raised his other hand slowly to my hair, pushing the sweaty strands back. The pleasure of a simple gesture like that shocked me. I tried to step away but found I couldn't.

His eyes flared in the dim light, and flames danced for a moment as I watched. Then he said, "I'm going to kiss you, Delaney. Because I can. And you don't have to worry about anything happening to me that I won't welcome. You can just enjoy it."

I opened my mouth to ask him to stop but his lips covered mine and I was lost in the feelings that roared up within me. He held me within the cage of his arms, strong but gentle at the same time. The taste of him was masculine and as he deepened the kiss, his soft lips pressing more firmly on mine, I relaxed into it, my eyes closing. Feelings rushed through me. I found myself struggling to keep my shields in place. It was so tempting to just give in and let them fall but I refused, unable to trust that it was safe.

His fingers swept up the sensitive skin of my spine. Even over the cotton of my shirt, the electricity of his touch left me breathless. Tickling flickers raced underneath my skin and my temperature soared suddenly, making my head swim. My knees wavered but Cal held me up, not allowing a break in contact as he pressed on with his experiment. His tongue tasted my bottom lip. I groaned at the feel of it, sagging against him. He pushed the advantage, exploring my mouth further until I fought back, twining my tongue with his.

His grip tightened around me in response, until there was no space separating us. We were pressed together, and I could feel the heat of his skin, radiating through his clothes and into me. I wanted to curl into that warmth.

That brought me back to reality, and I broke away from the kiss, even though every cell in my body screamed at me to get back to it. He kept his arm locked around me, not allowing me an escape. We stood there, leaning against each other, our hearts hammering in time.

"I've wanted to do that for a while." A sweet smile drifted across his face as he asked, "So, what'd you think?"

Stunned, my brain barely functioning, I tried to answer. "Wow," I squeaked out.

He laughed at my response and his happiness rumbled through me. Still pressed together, I could feel the thick weight of him hard against my leg. My excitement at the simple idea Cal could want me like that drove all other thoughts out of my head. I couldn't come up with anything else to say.

"Now that's the kind of response a guy likes to get when he kisses someone." He leaned in like he wanted to start the process again, but I pressed back in his arms, waving awkwardly between us.

"And is this the response a girl hopes to get when she kisses someone back?"

He laughed again, a wicked glint in his eyes. "Only when he really enjoys what's happening."

I grinned back, enjoying the moment. "Good answer, I think."

"It is. Definitely." He watched me, his face relaxed, his hands still gently skimming my back. "Did you feel your shields come down?" he asked.

My breath stopped. I hadn't noticed that at all. I'd been so used to keeping them in place all the time but sometime during the kiss, I'd lost track of everything except the heat between us.

"Don't panic. Your shields came down and I'm still here. Nothing bad happened."

His voice was reassuring, but I couldn't help but worry. "Do you feel any different? Like you just have to be with me? Can't stand the thought of being without me?"

His body shook with laughter, as he answered. "Oh, I

feel different right now. And yes, I absolutely want to be with you. Don't like the thought of going without you at all. But I don't think that has anything to do with your gift. I think I just like you."

I relaxed slightly at his teasing, realizing how inane my questions must have seemed. "Give me a chance here. My brain's a little scrambled after what we did."

"Oh honey, if you're shaken up by a kiss, just imagine how much more fun we could have." I shivered at the promise of those words.

I didn't try to contain my laughter. "I think I need to read romance novels now, if that's the kind of stuff it can teach me." His answering chuckle washed away any awkwardness I might have felt so I moved on with the matters at hand. "Now that you've sufficiently distracted me, we should probably talk about what happened out there."

He nodded, stepping away so we could talk. I ignored the fact that my body was unhappy with the new distance between us and focused on the task at hand.

"Do you know what a Golem is?" he asked.

"I know what you said when we were fighting it. Specifically made, given one purpose, which tells me it was sent here to attack us. But I don't understand who would have sent it."

He agreed. "That's part of the puzzle. There's also the question of how it was made. I've never known a Golem to come apart like that and then reform into small copies of itself. Usually, when you're able to disrupt their structural integrity, they disintegrate into inanimate pieces. This creature would have taken a lot of power to create."

"So, there's someone out there, bent on destroying us, that has a lot of magic at hand." I didn't like the idea of that, but all the evidence seemed to point in that direction.

Cal nodded. "That's the way it looks to me. This wasn't a standard Golem. There was something unusual mixed in with the clay, and I never saw the Naming it carried. I have no way to narrow down a list of suspects. But it has to be someone who isn't afraid to test magic and experiment."

"What's a Naming?" I asked. Something nagged at me, but I couldn't pin it down.

"To animate a Golem, you have to name it. Give it the Breath of Life. Usually, you'll write the name on the Golem's forehead as you form it. Or you'll have the name written on something, then put it inside the Golem. Without the name, a Golem won't function."

I closed my eyes and replayed the battle scene. I could see Callum taking the Golem down the first time, its pieces scattered about and even the smell came back to me. I wanted to gag but fought the urge. I played through the rest of the images, suddenly remembering the leathery object sticking out of the Golem's chest, just before it shifted and started to reform.

Opening my eyes, I said, "I saw something right after you knocked it down. It was sticking out from inside.

Looked like leather. I was about to pull it out when the copies began forming."

The attention on his face didn't bother me now. I appreciated that he was listening to me. Like we were partners trying to solve this problem together.

"That was probably it. Buried inside when it was made. The way it smelled tells me that its maker used animal fat of some kind, mixing that with the clay."

I remembered the odor in the air when I'd found the dead animals at the back end of my property. Too many coincidences were colliding.

"Your purification spell was a smart idea," said Callum, interrupting my thoughts. "Pretty sure that saved us all."

I shrugged. "Except for the fact that the explosion knocked Torren out. Seemed like a good idea up until then."

"That wasn't your fault, Laney."

"It was my idea to use that spell to kill the Golems. I feel a little responsible."

Cal shook his head. "You shouldn't. I realized at the last moment how intense the shock wave of that explosion could be. I threw up a shield around all of us, using the bracelets your father gave us as the focus. I didn't realize Torren wasn't wearing his, so he had no protection. If anyone is at fault for what happened to him, it's me."

Understanding hit me. While I'd been feeling responsible for what happened, so had Callum. But we'd both done all we could to try to protect each person in our little group.

I reached out to Cal, my fingers wrapping gently around his warm forearm. "We did what we could in a bad situation. If Torren had been wearing the bracelet like you'd told him to, he'd have been fine. But he didn't. We make the best of things as they are now and hope that they turn out all right."

As he listened, I could see the tension leaving him. "You're right. Thanks for ending my pity party before I could really get it started."

I smiled, feeling easier with him now. "Seems fair. You didn't let me enjoy mine for very long. I'm not about to let you wallow any longer. Let's get upstairs and figure out what we need to do next."

Chapter Thirty-Four

The shrill ringing of the phone woke me, jerking my head up off the table where I'd apparently laid it down a few short hours ago. My mouth was dry and tasted like acid as I coughed, "Hello," into the receiver.

"Ms. Murphy?" asked the alto voice on the other end of the line.

I nodded my head, then shook it, trying to wake myself up, thankful the caller couldn't see this painful process. "Yes," I answered. "Who's this?"

"This is Lana Kingston. We met in town the other day."

My brain clicked along, catching up with the conversation. "Yes, Sheriff. How are you?"

"Miss Tilly asked me to call you if anything happened."

"Which means something has happened."

The pause in her voice told me a lot, the stress she was feeling obvious to me even over the phone. "A young woman went missing last night."

"Oh no." I let the chair catch me and tried to remain calm. "Where was she from?"

"She's from Hazelwood. Maggie Adair. Do you know her?"

I pictured the young woman clearly in my mind. "Yes, of course. I've talked with her at her family's store. But how could she have gone missing? Hazelwood is well protected. I checked that myself."

"Her car was found on the highway, leading back to town. She'd been visiting some friends in Calhoun yesterday and when her family realized she wasn't in bed this morning, they went looking for her. The car was on the side of the road, about a hundred feet from the Hazelwood sign, with the driver's door standing wide open."

Realizing how close she'd been to safety, my heart sank. Whoever had taken Maggie knew about the stones and the protection they offered. "Any sign of what happened or where she was taken?" I hoped for good news but suspected the Sheriff Kingston had none to offer.

"Unfortunately, no. I'm afraid I have to go track down some more people to form a search party." She was professional, business-like, but I could feel the worry running beneath her voice.

"I'll wake up the guys and we'll come help. Where is everyone meeting?"

"No but thank you. You need to talk with Miss Tilly.

And if I'm right, I think you've got something coming your way you need to get ready for." Her news delivered, she hung up.

I put the phone back down and swiped at my eyes. Tears wouldn't help us now. Or Maggie. I had work to do.

Calling Miss Tilly, I was surprised when her granddaughter answered.

"Hello, Ms. Murphy. My grandmother said you would call. She asked me to give you a message."

"Are you sure I can't speak with her?"

"She's not here. She's meeting with people in town as we all try to locate Maggie. But she was adamant that you be given this message."

I took a deep breath and held it, worried about what I might hear.

"She said to tell you it's time. She's given you what you need already. Now you need to do what must be done."

The air rushed out of me as my head spun with confusion.

"Is that all, Aften? There must be more to what Miss Tilly wanted me to know."

"There is nothing else, Ms. Murphy. We all have jobs to do. We will do ours and you must do yours." With that said, she hung up on me, her task complete.

Hanging my head, I knew what Miss Tilly was trying to tell me. I just didn't want to admit that was the only option. Hearing movement, I turned to see Moose leaning his large head in through the doorway. His eyes were concerned as he padded toward me carefully.

I let my hand scratch gently at his ears for a moment, enjoying the silky feel of his black fur in this form. He leaned his head into my touch and the warmth of him filled me up. *"Friend,"* flashed through my mind and I looked down at him wondering. Callum had said you could hear a Hell Hound once you learned how to listen.

I patted him, scratched under his jaw and then said. "Moose, I need to talk to Cal for a bit. Can you get him for me? And then go check on Torren, please?"

With something like a nod, Moose left the room and I tried to turn my thoughts toward a plan. I briefly considered calling for Angus or Uncle Newt but forced myself to discard that idea. This mess was in my backyard, and I was going to be the one to clean it up.

I started laying out the things Miss Tilly had given me. If she was right, there was no time for me to waste. Night comes fast this time of year, and I needed to have everything ready to go.

I flicked on Cal's coffeemaker as he walked into the kitchen. A crease cut into his cheek from whatever he'd fallen asleep on and his hair was sticking up, but even that made my heart stutter a bit. He'd left his shirt behind and the hard muscles left exposed made me want to touch them. I turned away, focusing on the work in front of me. There was no time for what I wanted right now.

"You needed to talk to me?" he asked.

I nodded without turning around. "A woman from Hazelwood is missing. They found her car right outside of town. Search parties are forming to look for her."

"And you think this is related to the other women that were killed?"

"I do."

"Do you know this woman?"

"I've talked with her at her family's store in town. Briefly. That's all."

"Does she look like you?"

I closed my eyes, picturing Maggie Adair the last time I'd seen her. Months ago, maybe even a year. Her dark brown hair was long and we'd laughed about the fact that we wore the same size clothes. She'd been nice, her smile friendly. That's all I could remember.

"Delaney? Are you all right?" Cal's voice interrupted my thoughts, bringing me back to the problem at hand as his hand settled onto my shoulder.

"Yeah, I'm fine." I answered. "Maggie has brown hair. She's nice. Friendly. Which is probably what made her a target."

"But does she look like you?" he asked again, persistent.

I didn't like the answer I had for him. "No more than any of those other girls did." I didn't fight him as he gently turned me, his fingers lifting my chin up so my eyes met his.

"You carry this burden like you caused this. It's too

much. We will solve this problem and find Maggie." His voice was kind. I wanted to give in, to let him carry the weight. But I knew that wasn't for him to do. It really was on me. I just couldn't tell him that.

"I have some things I need to do to help Miss Tilly with the search. Can you check the perimeter for me? Make sure all the wards are still strong? After what happened with the Golem, I don't want to risk anything else getting through. We don't have time to deal with that right now."

"Of course. And I think we should call Angus. He'd want to know about this new progression of the threat against you."

That was exactly what we couldn't do. "I thought of that too, but you did say he and Uncle Newt are dealing with their own problems Below. We can handle this. As long as the wards are sound, we're safe here."

He sighed. "True. I hate not sharing information with him right away, but this would be a distraction for both of them. You promise to let him know if anything changes?"

I swallowed past the lump of truth wedged in my throat. My mother had worked so hard to teach me the importance of honesty, but right now it was easy to fall back on what I'd inherited from my father.

"Of course," I lied. "If anything changes, we'll contact him right away."

He looked down at me, his fingers touching my cheek in a fleeting gesture before he stepped back. "All right. I'll check the wards. You keep working in here and Moose will watch over Torren for us."

"How is he?" I asked, needing to know.

"He's better," said Cal. "Still unconscious but his breathing's improved and his heart rate's regular again. I think if we give him a few more days, he'll be fine."

I tried to smile, genuinely relieved to hear that someone close to me might survive the experience. "That's good news. I was afraid he might not wake up."

Cal offered me a reassuring smile in response. "You helped him. That was the difference. And once we finish this, you and I should work on ways you can have more control over your abilities. Maybe then, you won't feel you have to hide out here."

I couldn't hide the strain in my laugh. "Yes, we should work on that. Later."

"Soon," he said. "We'll find Maggie and the person who took her. We will end this and then we will turn all of our attention to you."

The way he said that made my stomach flip, but I didn't let it show. I turned back to the items I'd set out in specific order on the counter before me and started putting Miss Tilly's plan into action.

Chapter Thirty·Five

W HEN C ALLUM walked out the door to check our security, his hand lingered on my shoulder as he said goodbye. I couldn't help but watch him stride off, waiting until he was out of sight before I got back to work. I ignored the voice in my head that told me I could do this another way, shutting it out and focusing on what had to be done.

As the time passed, I poured all my energy into preparing the herbs Miss Tilly had sent home with me. Layering them carefully together exactly as instructed, I boiled and mixed them as needed, then let them rest in cold water. I swiped at the nervous sweat that kept rolling down my face. This had to come together perfectly, or it could all fall apart.

My father's arrival in the kitchen as I labored over the hot stove was heralded with a shift in the pressure around me that made me want to shake my head and sneeze until my ears popped. I shoved the written instructions I'd been following into a pocket, turning around to face him just as he stepped out of the portal he'd used.

Angus glanced at my tired face, worry lining his eyes before he reached for me. Pulling me into a quick embrace, he cupped my jaw and looked down. "You look like you're toiling over a cauldron. Miss Tilly's work, I assume?"

I nodded, dancing around him to guide his attention away from what I had been crafting. "She's been trying to teach me a few things. How to see clearly, how to cast a Truth Telling, that sort of thing."

"Herb magic. She's always had that talent. Nothing wrong with you learning what she's willing to teach."

"Glad you approve."

He smiled, a little baring of teeth in that motion. "I don't think it would matter to you if I approved or not, Laney. You'll do what you think is best either way."

"Like letting me live out here alone?" I asked. Maybe this was his way of calling back the bodyguards, an idea which saddened me a little.

"No. Nothing like that. There's too much danger right now for you to be without protection. But Callum has told me good things since he's been here. I hope you'll listen to him. He can teach you a lot."

All I could do was nod, not trusting myself to say anything about what he'd taught me already. Changing the subject seemed wise. "Did he call you here today?"

"Yesterday. He wanted me to know about the Golem. He also told me what happened to Torren. That's why I'm here. I wanted to check on him and on you, make sure that his condition wasn't weakening you."

"It's not. I've felt fine. Cal said he's stabilized, and I've got Moose watching over him for me now."

"Good. And you like the Hound?" The tone in his voice surprised me, almost like he was hoping I liked a gift he'd given me.

"He's great Dad. I wish you'd just told me that he was coming instead of making him pretend to be a regular dog. But he seems happy here." Truthfully, it was difficult for me to think of a time when Moose wouldn't be here with me. The idea of it made the house seem emptier immediately. And colder.

"You know I've never been one to choose a straight line when other options were available. I wasn't sure how welcoming you'd be to a Hell Hound on your doorstep. Getting him in the door was important. If you grew to appreciate him, even better."

That was truth, carefully put. With Angus, there could be anything happening behind that rock star facade; plans and schemes, circling and coinciding, even clashing sometimes. Especially around those he loved.

"How's Uncle Newt?" I asked, still trying to keep his attention distracted.

"He's away right now." When I looked at him for more details, Angus just said, "On business."

I shook my head but didn't say anything else. If he wanted me to know more, he'd either tell me or expect me to figure it out on my own. At my silence, Angus reached for my hand, his long graceful fingers folding gently around mine. It reminded me of how he'd tried to teach me to play guitar, his fingers deft on the strings, mine always a shade too small to make the same magic he did.

"You're really all right?" His question was careful but there was an urgency below it that I'd rarely heard from him. He needed to hear me say the words.

"I am Daddy. I promise." The softness of my answer seemed to reassure him and he relaxed, the minute tension of his jaw easing. I hadn't noticed that clench before it receded.

"I have to go. But we'll talk again when we both have more time. Be careful with yourself."

"I will." Before he could leave, I had to pass a message along. I'd been keeping it from him, afraid of how the words might hurt him. But this might be my last chance to share it with him. "Hey. Mom wanted you to know she's good now." I tried to say the words gently, but he flinched anyway.

"You've talked to her? She's doing well?"

I nodded. "She also said you need to know she doesn't blame you. She never did. She wants you to find a way to forgive yourself for everything that happened."

With those words, my father turned away, distance growing with each step as he prepared to leave me. Just before the portal snapped shut, the rush of air carried his voice to me. "Easier said than done, Love."

CHAPTER THIRTY·SIX

WITH ANGUS GONE, the house became too quiet and my skin itched with discomfort. I returned to my task, letting the mundane activity of following directions distract me from the worries gnawing at my mind. Work was something easy to do, a way to avoid thinking of how much I had to lose if this went wrong. I moved from one item to another, ignoring what was coming for now.

By the time Cal had returned from his extensive check of our security, the result of my efforts was cooling in the fridge behind a jug of milk. I handed him a cup of coffee almost automatically as he walked in. In such a short span of time, I'd learned his routine and the things he liked.

He sipped the brew, his smile grateful. "Things look good out there. The areas the Hound and I built up are holding and the stones are strong. As long as you're within the borders, you're safe. Assuming you'll stay within those lines."

It was an almost question, hopeful in its way. "I'll do my best. If someone needs me, I'm not going to hide in here."

He didn't say anything, just laid a gentle hand on my arm as I started past him. When I looked at him, he searched my face, eyes roving over me, looking for something I was afraid he'd see. I stayed still, letting him look. Wondering if he might actually see something he liked in me.

When he released me, I moved on to the job of cleaning up the pans and utensils I'd used in my work. While I scrubbed, he slowly drained his coffee, filling the cup back up when it was empty. Needing to break the silence, I said, "Angus was here while you were out."

"Oh. Was there something he needed?"

"Not really. He said he wanted to check in on me and see how Torren was."

"Ah. The worried father."

I laughed but it felt brittle. "Something like that, I guess. He did say you've told him good things about my skills." I paused, needing to say this the right way. "Thank you for that. I want him to know I can take care of myself. He doesn't have to worry all the time."

I heard Cal moving behind me, could feel the air shrinking between us as he got closer. His voice was soft when he answered. "I didn't do it as a favor to you. Or to him. It was simply the truth." Then a teasing tone slid into his voice. "Doesn't mean you don't still have a lot to learn.

And I told him I'd be happy to stick around for a while longer to teach you a few more things."

I coughed to hide the pain I felt building inside me. "Glad I haven't scared you off yet."

He was so close behind me I could feel the loose hairs on my neck shift when he spoke this time. "Laney, I can feel there's something you're not telling me. What is it?"

I grasped for an answer that would appease him. "My mom asked me to give Angus a message. I don't think he took it very well."

"Oh. I understand." From his tone, it sounded like he meant it. "He loves her still, you know."

I didn't say anything. I didn't need to. This was another truth we both knew. I also knew that sometimes, not even love was enough to save someone. I swiped at an errant tear that escaped my eye. "Enough of that. Work to be done. I best get to it."

As I tried to turn and go around him, Cal leaned in and put his arms on the counter, trapping me. The warmth of him flowed into me and the chill I'd been carrying around inside since I'd heard from Miss Tilly threatened to thaw. "We'll get through this, you know."

"How can you know that?" I felt desperation clawing up from my stomach, wanting to believe him.

"I just do. We're all a team now." He held up his wrist, the leather he wore tying him to me. His lips brushed over my forehead, fleeting. I wanted to pull him in closer and take more of what he offered in that simple kiss but forced myself not to. Instead I nodded and put a smile on my face.

"You're right. I think I'll go check on Torren now so Moose can take a break."

He stepped back, giving me room to move away. "Good idea. I'll take the Hound outside so he can stretch his legs. See if there's anything he notices that I might have missed."

Clearing them out of the house gave me a few undisturbed moments to think. Knowing what Miss Tilly wanted me to do, I felt sick. The spell she'd given me was powerful. My stomach twisted at the idea of what it would do to the ones I was surprised to find I cared about.

"You're not a hard-hearted person, Delaney. That's why you're out here in the first place. To limit the number of people you could end up caring about." Talking to myself helped me process the way I was feeling. I also recognized most people would consider me crazy if they could hear the conversation.

And crazy is undoubtedly what someone would think if they could hear the answering voice in my head, the one that reminded me of my mother telling me something important. "Worrying won't get this job done girl. Chin Up. It's gonna be all right."

Checking in on Torren, I was relieved to see he looked much better. His color had improved and his breathing seemed easier. I squeezed his fingers and was shocked to get a response. As his fingers tightened on mine, the air between us shivered, a high sound ringing out. Closing my eyes and focusing inward, I saw the bright lines connecting us pulsing in rhythm. They looked healthy and whole, giving me hope that Torren might really be on the path to recovery.

I couldn't resist the urge to run my fingers over his soft hair. A sigh escaped him at my touch and his lips almost curved in a smile. Guilt surged up inside me as I thought about what had happened between Cal and me earlier, while Torren was resting upstairs, recovering from an injury he sustained because of me.

"I need you to be okay, Torren." I whispered the words, praying that he would hear them on some level.

He shifted under my fingers. "I think at this point, you can call me Tor."

I leaned away from him, surprised by the sound of his voice. His eyes were barely open, but they tracked my movement. He tried to lift himself up, but pain flashed across his face and he stopped, breathing heavily with the effort.

"Fair enough. I'll call you Tor, if you rest and get better." I teased him easily, happy he was conscious and talking. He nodded, his eyes closing again as he relaxed. His fingers released mine and I stood to go. While it cheered me to think I'd been able to speed his possible recovery, my heart hurt when I admitted that he was here, in danger, because of me. Finding a way to end this mess for all of us was a priority. I patted his arm, whispered a goodbye and went to my room to change into warmer clothes. It was going to be cold and I planned to be ready for what was coming.

CHAPTER THIRTY·SEVEN

By the time Callum and Moose found their way back, I had a quick dinner pulled together. I'd worked the ingredients Miss Tilly had given me into a sauce, the delicious scent of beef filtering through the kitchen. I put some treats in a bowl for Moose and covered them with the sauce I'd left chilling in the fridge, softening the crunchy bite sized pieces. Moose sniffed at the food cautiously, then began eating, wolfing the pieces down.

Cal nodded his thanks as he examined the food in front of him. I'd soaked the meat for his sandwich in the mayo-looking sauce as well and waited as Cal took a bite.

"This is really good," Cal said, after he'd swallowed down several large bites. "Thank you."

Words wouldn't come, so I waved his thanks off like it was nothing. I nibbled at my food, hoping my nervousness wasn't as obvious as I was afraid it was.

Still, Cal picked up on something. "Delaney, what's wrong?"

I shook my head. "Nothing. Just worried about Maggie."

"You know you can tell me if there's a problem. Let me help."

I closed my eyes at those words. "I know, but this is something I need to figure out on my own."

He pushed back his chair to stand and I whispered, "Stop."

Cal froze as that single word left my mouth and pain blossomed in my chest. Moose growled and started toward me. I turned immediately to him and in a soft voice said, "Lay down." He collapsed onto the floor, a sad whine escaping him as he realized he had no control over himself. Tears pricked at my eyes but I swiped them away. The next words hurt as I forced them out. "You will both stay here tonight. You will not call anyone. You will not come after me."

The stunned looks on their faces burned into my memory as I left them behind. Racing down the stairs to the basement, I pulled on the coat I'd hidden behind the door. I tried to ignore the tears running down my face, wiping my nose on my sleeve. Nothing could forgive what I'd just done. It was only temporary, but they were still held there against their will. The only comfort I could hold onto was that Torren would be taken care of. If I didn't make it back tonight, they would clean up the mess for me. Somehow.

Miss Tilly had made a quick call earlier that evening, letting me know that she and Aften had tracked Maggie to an old farmhouse not far from my property. It had been abandoned years ago and was hidden from view by a stand of trees. They were sure she was being kept there. It was my job alone to get her back.

I slunk down the tunnel between my house and the garage. Climbing up through the trapdoor, I fought the shiver that hit me and refused to give in to the worries that threatened to overwhelm me. Put one foot in front of the other. That's all I had to do.

I lingered over my father's red Mustang convertible, running my hands along the smooth paint he still babied when he visited. I'd kept this car for him, knowing how much he loved it. I opened the door, leaving the envelope from my back pocket on the seat. I didn't need to put his name on it. He'd know what it was and by the time he found it, I'd be gone.

Opening the door of my own car, I felt a sad smile crease my face. I could almost hear Angus laughingly say, "My little Hellcat," as I slid behind the wheel. The fact that I'd chosen Plum Crazy Purple over his favored flame red was something he'd never forget. I hoped when he remembered, that it was a happy thing for him.

I pressed the button and the garage door rolled up, my getaway fast with no one to stop me. I glanced back at my home once, only. The lights blazed behind me, looking like nothing had changed. I didn't allow myself anything else, ignoring the reflection in the mirror as I focused on the road ahead.

I let the engine open up on the gravel road, miles flying by as I left a dusty haze hanging behind. If this was going to be my last drive, I was going to enjoy every bit of it. I gunned it, relishing the feel as the car leapt beneath me, power vibrating up into my hands on the wheel. I slid around corners I could hardly see in the darkness, driving more by feel than anything. Those rare moments of flight as I crested a hill were glorious and heart stopping. Miss Tilly had warned everyone off these roads and my way was clear. The only things I had to watch for were deer and the turns I needed to make.

Chapter Thirty-Eight

THERE ARE a lot of empty old farmhouses scattered around Nebraska, beautiful and eerie all at once, especially in the moonlight. The one Miss Tilly gave me directions to was exactly those things. The white clapboard siding shone, the chipped and faded paint not so visible with the surrounding darkness. The once graceful details that adorned the fascia and railings were allowed a brief return to their former glory once the sun went down. Even the ancient wood shakes on the roof gleamed silver, and I could hear the front screen door bang every time the wind swirled along the wraparound porch. There was no light inside but there was a watchfulness in the cold air. Someone was in there, waiting for me.

I slid out of my car, letting my hands caress the soft leather one more time before I left it all behind. It was time to face my fears. To be a good person. Stop evil where I could. Sacrifice myself if need be. The woman being hidden here would go home to her family. She had to.

I stepped up onto the old porch. It sagged with age, the wood creaking beneath my feet. I pushed open the unlatched front door, assaulted by the stale air inside. The moon's glow lit the interior enough that I wasn't entirely blind. To the right was what had once been a dining room, a grand space I could imagine filled with family and laughter. Now, it was empty and silent, the weight of memories piled up in the space.

A disturbance in the air to my left caught my attention. I turned in that direction, taking cautious steps from the entry into a large open room. The dust danced in the air and I could see a figure seated on a sagging couch along the far wall, long legs folded at uncomfortable angles. When he stood, I gasped. My heart stuttered in recognition. I knew this man. His straight blond hair was greasy, making me wonder when he'd last had a shower and his clothes hung on his thin frame. He'd been vibrant and strong when I'd last seen him. The changes in him from then to now made my heart hurt and I tried to catch my breath to say something. To say anything at all.

"Hello Delaney," he whispered, his voice rough. He gestured at the space around him, as if he was welcoming me into his own home. "So glad you could join us tonight."

"Brett," I said, hating the shake in my voice but making no attempt to hide it.

"I wondered if you'd ever find your way here. Or if you'd ever care about someone else enough to even look."

I chose to ignore the barb and got to the most important thing on tonight's agenda. "Where is she?"

"No, no. That's not how we do this." Brett shook his head as he reached out to me, trailing his finger along my arm. "We've been apart too long. I want to hear about everything you've done since you left me. Everything."

I refused to recoil from his touch, enduring it. "You're the one who tracked me down. You must already know what I've been doing."

"You've done more than you're willing to admit to anyone." He paused, silence adding to the tension filling the room around us. "Like in Angel Falls. Now, that was impressive."

I closed my eyes, the confirmation that he had been there truly breaking my heart.

"That man was hurting women, Brett. He needed to be stopped."

His voice was harsh this time, his anger intent on me. "That man was my friend. He helped me."

"That doesn't mean what he was doing was right." I purposely kept my voice soft, hoping there was a way to lead him back to reason. "You know me. You know I could never stand by and watch someone be hurt. I had to step in."

"I was hurt. Where were you when I needed you?"

Agony coated his words. I wouldn't lie to him. I made

sure to keep my voice calm, hoping I could soothe some of the pain he'd held since our high school prom. "If I'd stayed, things would have only gotten worse for you. For everyone. I left because I had to." I took a step closer to him, reaching up to where his hand still rested against my arm. His indrawn breath told me it was the right thing to do. I pressed my advantage. I unlocked my magic, allowing the smallest bit to wrap itself around my voice, coaxing him. "And I know that you want to do the right thing too. So tell me, please, where is Maggie?" I used her name, wanting to remind him that she was a person with a life waiting for her away from these problems we had created.

Brett's hand grabbed mine, bruising and angry. "Now, that disappoints me. All this time and you don't even want to catch up. Right to what *you* want." His grip on my hand tightened as he spoke, a vise that wasn't going to release me.

"Why are you doing this, Brett? I don't believe this is something you want to do. Not really." I couldn't help but question him, even though I feared I already knew the answer.

His words pummeled me, fast and harsh. "Because you left me. Left me with nothing. Left me in that place."

"I left because I believed it would be better for you. I was trying to help you."

He swung me around. The sudden movement had me backpedaling, trying to maintain my balance. He pulled me close, my back against his chest. He'd grown so thin, I could feel the sharp lines of his ribs as he sucked in a pained breath. "Help me? Help me! They couldn't do anything for me. I needed you and you left me behind, alone."

I forced myself to focus, desperately fighting the sudden flare of desire that threatened to overwhelm me at his touch. Even after all this time, we were still tied together. I shivered in his arms, but still hoped that I could make him understand. Maybe since I was there with him, the madness I was sensing in him would ease. This didn't have to end badly.

"Brett." My voice was soft and I layered power into every word. Power loaded with happy memories of warm, sunlit days. Times we'd spent laughing, a reminder of our friendship that had turned into something more. "Please listen to me. I was poisoning you. When I left, I was trying to save you."

His eyes gleamed as he bared his teeth at me. "Poison? Yes, that's exactly what you are. My poison. But you were wrong about one thing. I didn't want to be saved. I don't NEED to be saved. I'm better this way and now you're here. You're mine again." His put his mouth right next to my ear and I flinched away before I could stop myself. "When you left, there was a hole in me that constantly ached. Nobody in the hospital could understand why I needed you. They just shoved drugs into me until I stopped talking about it. I couldn't make them understand how deep my pain was, what real longing felt like. They were used to dealing with crazy people. But I couldn't make them see I wasn't crazy."

I winced as a memory of that pain hit him, traveling to me, almost stopping my heart for a brief moment, before it started up again. To go through that, over and over again.

"I'm sorry. I was trying to do the right thing."

He shoved me away and I stumbled, tripping over my own feet. I landed on the couch, the ancient cushions groaning. I knew I could fight him, take him down and put a quick end to this. Despite his height, he was emaciated, his muscles weakened. I calculated multiple ways I could overpower him but even now, I didn't want to hurt him. I could take a few bumps and bruises if it let him calm down, made him believe he was in control. I had to find a way to reach the good man I believed still existed under this sickness.

He stalked toward me, a feral look on his face. I forced myself to focus on his eyes instead of searching the room for ways to escape.

"When I was waiting for you, hurting and praying you'd come back, a man came to my room one night. He promised that if I told the doctors what they needed to hear, he'd make sure I was released. He'd help me get better. And that's what he did."

"What man?" I asked. "Are you talking about the man in Angel Falls?"

Brett twitched, like my question bothered him. "No, no. Can't talk about the man. But my friend. Yes, you killed him."

"I don't understand."

My words just made him angrier. "What don't you understand? You killed my friend. Now, I have to do this all on my own."

Worry sparked but I had to follow this through. I made my voice soft. "What do you have to do? Maybe I can help you?"

"You can't. You can't help with this. I'll finish this and then you'll come with me."

"But what if I can help? You won't know until you talk to me. I've learned a lot since we've been apart."

He shook his head, his lank hair flopping. "I'm not telling you anything until I know you're going to stay with me. That no one came with you. That you're mine."

"Brett, I'm here with you now. Just you and me. I'm not running away. But you know me so well. You know I'd never be able to stay if something happened to the woman you're hiding."

He knelt in front of me, down on one knee. A crazed joy lit his face as he looked up. The twisted image of him as a hopeful groom made me nauseous. He grabbed my left hand tightly, bruising the skin and grinding the bones together painfully. He shoved a metal circle onto my ring finger and the icy bite of it burned my flesh, its coldness quickly penetrating. My hand cramped in reaction and the sour tang of the magic in the ring coated my tongue, making me gag.

"Now," he said, his voice choked with emotion as he gave me a jubilant smile, his eyes shining. "Now you're really mine! The man promised and made me learn, but now you're bound to me. Just like I've been bound to you."

I didn't have to fake my confusion. "What man are you talking about and what exactly is this? It really hurts, Brett. Do you want to hurt me?"

I tried to keep my voice soothing, but inside my mind was whirling. Someone who knew something of binding magic had told him to do this, had given him a token he thought would tie us together. Already I could feel the magic trying to burrow its way inside me, to take control, but all the time I'd spent shielding myself from others was proving useful. At the moment, I was winning the battle. Exactly how long I could hold out was questionable and depended a lot on things I didn't know. How strong was the magic woven into this piece of metal? How long could I divide my attention before my shields started to slip?

Brett's eyes were narrowed, watching me like he didn't fully believe what I was saying. A shard of pain shot through my left palm and I gasped, my hand convulsing in his grip. The grimace on my face must have communicated the truth of what I was saying, and his face became concerned.

"It's not supposed to hurt. It's just to help you love me. That's what I was promised." He seemed almost childlike, trying to puzzle through the problem before him.

"Brett, you don't need this to make me love you," I said, whispering to him, his face so close to mine that I could kiss him if I wanted to.

As he watched me, I let my eyes fill with tears, feeling him search through our old connection until he found something that satisfied him. I stayed silent and still, letting him examine me inside and out, believing in the words I'd said because, at some level, they were true.

Eventually, he nodded and gave me a smile, one that reminded me of the boy he'd once been. The boy who'd held my hand and given me the same grin just before my very first kiss. He tugged on the ring and pulled it off my finger, and I heard it hit the wood planks of the floor and roll away. The cramping pain in my hand relaxed and the metallic taste in my mouth tapered off. I let him pull me up off the couch and into an embrace. Ignoring the smell of him, I laid my head on his chest. He began to rock back and forth, humming a song I didn't know.

"Please, Brett, it's time," I said. "We need to let Maggie go home. Where is she? You know, her family is missing her just as much as I missed you."

He nodded, and dropped his arms, grabbing my right hand to pull me down the hallway and up the rickety stairs. Some of the boards were loose and I stumbled over one as I tried to keep up with him. On the second floor, he led me into a bedroom, a crumpled body on the floor.

The girl at my feet was wearing a dress I knew instantly. I gasped at the sight. I'd donated it when I first came to Hazelwood, needing to purge myself of the things that reminded me of what had happened before.

Brett nodded, a satisfied look on his face after seeing my astonishment and recognition. "She's wearing your dress. She shouldn't be wearing that. That's why I took her. I wanted you to have it back. You're the only one who should ever wear this special dress. You remember, when I asked you to go to prom with me? I was so nervous and you kept teasing me, asking me what was wrong. I'd never been so happy as I was when you said yes that day."

It was too dark for me to see if Maggie was breathing so I knelt carefully down beside her, resting my hand on her chest, reassured when I felt the shallow rise and fall. She was still alive. There was blood on her face and what might have been a large gash above her right eye, but she was alive. That was all that mattered to me.

"This is good," I said to Brett, turning to him with an attempt at a smile on my face. "She can go home and we can start over."

He shook his head in response, standing over me, hands fisted at his sides. "No. We can't let her go."

"Brett, we can't keep her here. She has a family that loves her. She lives with her parents and her younger brother and sister. They're waiting for her to come home. They need her to come home."

He looked confused. "But, I kept her here for you. So we can do this together. Prove how much you still love me."

Something twisted in my chest, a knife sharp bite of pain making it hard to breathe. I didn't want to have to make this choice. "Brett, we don't have to do this. We're not killers. We can forget about all this and go back to who we were before. I've missed you for so long, how kind you always were. We can leave here, together, if you'll let Maggie go."

He was conflicted, his eyes flitting between me and Maggie on the floor. In the near darkness, I'm sure we looked a lot alike. He finally relaxed, and I felt like I'd won her freedom.

He reached for my hand, pulling me up with him. He leaned in and I let him kiss me despite his rancid breath. When we broke apart, I didn't wipe my mouth as I longed to do. He gazed down at me, almost happy, but then his eyes narrowed again. Madness reappeared.

"No, she can't go. She's seen me. If she tells anyone, they'll take me away from you. And it'll be like before. It will be even worse."

I tried to calm him. "Brett, I can make her forget you. I know how to do that. She'll never know who you were. They won't find us." The words fell out of me, lies I tried to cover with soothing magic. I hated deceiving him, but I wasn't willing to sacrifice Maggie. She had to survive this.

He spun away from me, ignoring my attempt to find the words that would ease his fears. "No!" he screamed. "I won't let them tear us apart again. She'll die and then we'll start over."

Keeping my body between him and Maggie, I didn't try to keep the shaking out of my voice this time, didn't hide the tears that were starting to fall. "Please Brett. Please. I can't let something happen to her because of me. You don't have to do this."

He prowled toward us, intent on the unconscious woman on the floor. I knew I couldn't wait anymore. I had to do what I'd been afraid of all along, what I'd promised myself I would never do. I'd left everything I loved behind and isolated myself to make sure this never happened. But he left me no other choice. I grabbed him as he tried to step around me and pulled him off balance. He grasped my arms in an attempt to steady himself, but I pressed forward with my offense. I pulled his head down, kissing his lips fully and dropping my shields completely at the same time. The blackness inside him roared into me. I gave in and welcomed it, letting it coat my insides with a slimy filth that made me want to retch. There, in that empty shell of what was once a home, with what might be a dying girl at my feet and a man I might have been able to love if things had been different, I drained Brett of every bit of energy he had, gulping down his life with every swallow. He fought me at first, but I held on, never breaking contact with him. I held on against his every attempt to push me away, to wrench his lips from mine. I held on until he sagged against me, until I could feel that his heart no longer beat, and his skin began to chill under my fingers.

When I was sure he was truly gone I gently laid him down on the bare floor, next to the woman he'd wanted to kill. Tears streamed down my face as the pain of not being able to save Brett hit me. I crawled over to the corner and vomited until there was nothing left inside me. That's how Angus found me, next to a pile of stinking sick, my knees drawn up and sobbing.

Chapter Thirty-Nine

I WOKE in my own bed, flannel sheets and heavy blankets a cocoon of warmth. The wind was howling outside, grumbling thunder came and went. Uncle Newt sat in the cozy chair across the room, a soft light on next to him. Even with his stillness, I knew he was awake and watching me. When I tried to sit up, he stood and came to help me, propping me with pillows. I felt faded, but realized I was at least clean. Someone had bathed me and wrestled me into a soft shirt and sweatpants.

"Glad you decided it was time to wake up," Newt said, patting my cheek gently. "We've been worried."

"Was I out for a while?"

"It's been a full day since Angus brought you home."

"What about Maggie? Brett's body?" After everything I'd done to try to save her, I was afraid it hadn't been enough.

Newt nodded. "Maggie is fine. The sheriff's office

received an anonymous call with the location of where she was being held. She was treated at the hospital for exposure and a head injury, then sent home with her family. She doesn't recall anything after stopping outside Hazelwood when she saw a young man trying to help an injured dog. She said they talked for a minute, he asked about a vet because he felt bad for hitting it with his car. She remembers giving the young man directions. That's it. When her parents got to the hospital, she told them she was just trying to be nice."

"And Brett?" I asked.

"His body was next to her, right where you left him. According to the coroner, he had a weak heart. He was malnourished and dehydrated. All of that, and the stress of what he'd done, was too much for his body. His heart simply gave out before he could kill her. That's the official version of things."

I couldn't bring myself to look at him. "You know that was me. I did that to him." I tried to keep my voice strong, but it wavered anyway.

Newt pushed his way into my line of vision, sitting down next to me on the mattress. "I know that. We all do. We also know you only did it to stop him from hurting anyone else. But Hells, you were in bad shape when Angus got you back here, Laney. Not to mention, I thought your father was going to tear the world apart when he realized what you'd decided to do. You can't put yourself and everyone else at risk like that."

I couldn't meet his eyes, so I stared at the top of the blanket covering me, twisting my hands in its softness. "I did what I believed was right, Newt. I hoped you at least would understand that."

His hands stopped mine, gripping them kindly but firmly, forcing me to look at him. "I do understand. That doesn't mean I agree with you. I know how afraid you are, down deep, that someone might suffer because of you. I know you feel you have to prevent that at all costs." I sat silently, nothing to offer, no argument to be made. He was right.

"Forget everything you think could happen for a moment. Just let all that go and think about what the world would be like for each one of us without you in it. You matter to people. Whether you believe me, or you don't, I don't care. You matter." When I tried to interrupt him, he silenced me with a familiar look. "No. No arguing. You matter to people. I know you've tried very hard to avoid that, to prevent that from happening. But what's done is done. People care about you. Not because of some irresistible magic spell or power. It's because of who you are."

I couldn't stop the unexpected sobs when they broke free of my control. My shoulders were shaking as tears rolled down my face, snot running out of my nose.

Uncle Newt waited, letting me cry for a while. When I finished, he handed me tissues and stayed silent while I wiped my face as clean as I could. He watched me, a sad smile on his worn face. "And if you won't believe what I've told you, then remember this. There is ruthlessness in your father. Darkness. It's been held in check since he met your mother, since you were born. But it's still there. And it truly will be Hell on Earth if anything happens to either of you. Stop making yourself a target."

I froze at those words. I didn't know the part of my father he was describing but I clearly remembered the nightmare I'd had. "By the way, where is Angus?" I asked. "I expected him to be here yelling at me, maybe even threatening me with a warm, cozy room in a Hell of his choosing." I was trying to joke, to make light of things, but we both knew it was a feeble attempt.

A flicker along his jaw worried me. This was the stoic face I'd seen every time he had bad news to share. "Once we could see you were safe and going to live, he had to leave. There are troubling things happening Below and he's got to be there to maintain the upper hand. That's what he's had me working on so much. That's why he sent you the Hound and Callum."

"Really? I thought they were just here to be my babysitters since you weren't available."

Newt shook his head. "No, they're here to protect you. Angus hoped you'd develop a bond with them, that you would be less lonely having them here. But ultimately, their job was to protect you. Whether you wanted them to or not."

I'd done exactly the thing my father had been trying to prevent. "Are Cal and Moose in trouble because of me?"

The silence between us was tense, making me afraid of what Newt had to tell me. "You left the evidence of what you'd done to them in clear view, so they won't be punished." Newt's voice changed, warning me. "But I don't think you'll find it so easy if you attempt it again. You hurt them when you did this. You might want to start with an apology. And don't expect them to be so willing to eat whatever you make for them in the future."

All I could do was nod. I'd betrayed my closest friends. I had to find a way to make things right with them.

"You need to understand their job is bigger than just keeping you from getting into trouble. There are beings in this world that see you as a tool to be used against Angus. Now, with the power you displayed when you decided to save that woman, they'll see you as a valuable weapon. Callum and the Hound have been assigned the job of keeping you from anyone who would try to use you against your father."

I swallowed. That sounded ominous. "To what extent? Are we talking death? My death?" I had been so prepared to sacrifice myself and almost welcomed the end when I'd thought it was my choice, but the idea of someone else scripting it for me had me on the edge of anger. Anger tinged with fear.

Newt walked away from me to lean against the wall

where the shadows gathered. I couldn't see his face, but his voice was sure and strong. "Your father loves you very much. But what you did, the way you put yourself in danger has made him rethink things."

"What do you mean?"

"If you're going to be in the middle of everything, you need to be more prepared. Cal will be training you full time now. There will be no more working for the Foundation. You must be able to defend yourself against whatever is coming. Those are your father's orders."

He stayed quiet, watching snow fall outside my window, as I absorbed all the information. I'd already been told that my very presence in this world would destroy it. Now I was being told that if something happened to me, the very thing I'd been trying to prevent would happen anyway. And Angus was already trying to fight a battle for control of Hell—he didn't need to be worrying about me while he dealt with that.

But there was a bigger problem looming over us all. Brett's death hadn't really solved anything.

"Newt?"

He turned to me. "Yes."

"Brett wasn't working alone in this."

"What do you mean?"

"Well, when I went to the farmhouse, he was so weak and scattered; I couldn't believe he'd orchestrated all these things. The Proles demon that attacked me here, the different women that were killed and displayed to look like me. Then he mentioned some man visited him in the hospital and told him what he should do so we could be together again. They'd been working together all this time. He even had a ring with binding magic in it that he put on my finger. If you hadn't taught me to shield, I think the magic would've forced an even stronger bond."

"Binding magic built into a ring? That's rare." He sounded concerned, even though I knew he was trying to hide it.

"The question is, who would have known to come after me by using Brett? I never told anyone about him or what happened."

Newt was following my train of thought. "The case received a lot of publicity. Your name, the ties back to Angus. It was all over the media for a long time. Your mother handled that as best she could while you were with us Below."

"But how did they find him at the hospital? And why?"

"I don't know. But it's something worth checking out. If I find anything, I'll let you or Cal know." He kissed me on the forehead, handing me a heavy case. "You should open this. Then you have some work to do around here." He moved away to the far wall, stepping back into the tunnel he'd opened, the heat ruffling my hair and the bed sheets before the opening snapped shut.

I leaned back against the pillows, closing my eyes as I thought about everything that had happened. I hadn't told Newt the worst of it. When I'd stolen Brett's life, I'd seen flashes of his memories. I'd seen the truth. Brett hadn't killed any of the girls that had died. He'd been there. He'd lured them in. But he hadn't been the one to murder them. That had been someone else. A man whose face I never could see. I'd destroyed Brett. I'd been the reason this all began. Then I killed him.

There was a tightness in my chest, but I refused to give in to the despair. I looked at the case Newt had given me, unlatching it. Inside was a piece of paper with my name scrawled across it in my father's handwriting.

Pushing aside the packing, I sucked in a gasp. A forty-caliber handgun rested inside, the metal flashing a deep purple as I held it up to the light. The weight of it fit comfortably in my hand, like it belonged there.

"There are blessed bullets you'll need to use with that."

I turned toward that deep voice, wincing at the way Cal held himself back from me. He stood just inside my doorway. Moose hovered behind him, eyes drooping sadly.

I put the package from Angus aside, getting out of my bed and eating up the distance between us. I threw my arms around his neck and hung on, the steel in his resistance making me ache.

"I'm sorry Cal. I'm so sorry."

He took my hands in his, pulling them free when I tried to hold on and pushing me away. "You should have trusted me. Trusted us."

I had to help him understand. "It's not that I didn't trust

either of you." I let my gaze encompass both him and Moose. "It wasn't that at all. But I had to do this alone. If I hadn't, I was afraid Maggie would have died before we could even try to save her."

"You don't know that. If you'd given us a chance to plan, we could have been there, hiding, ready to help you when you needed it. You should have given us that chance."

"Cal, look at me, please." I waited until his eyes met mine, stunned by the sadness I saw there. "If we had done that, I wouldn't have found out what I needed to know. There is someone out there, trying to hurt me, trying to hurt Angus. He's trying to use people I care about. Words can't fix what I did, but I need you both to know I did it because I believed it was the only way I could keep you safe."

Moose whined, coming closer now, rubbing his nose against my leg. Callum didn't look away from me, but the way his jaw clenched told me he was still angry.

"Will you stay with me? Both of you?" I had to ask, to give them the option to stay or to go.

"Angus has ordered us to stay. He believes you still need us." Cal's words cut into me, nothing I didn't deserve. He was here because Angus told him he had to be.

"It doesn't matter to me if Angus has given you orders or not. You know I won't keep someone here against their will. If you want to go, I will make Angus release you. It's your choice." I kept my voice even, refusing to let my hope that they'd choose to stay show.

Cal wasn't going to let that go. "Laney, what do you want?"

I wrapped my arms around him again, resting my forehead against his chest. "I want you both to stay. Please." Moose whined again, and I felt the nudge he gave Cal. I held my breath, waiting for his decision.

He sighed before answering me. "We'll stay. As long as you're willing to make a promise that you won't abandon us like that again. We're a team. We work together. No more running off to put yourself in danger."

I nodded, relieved, enjoying his warmth as it soaked into me. His arms came up, surrounding me and I gave in, nurturing the hope that maybe we'd get through this somehow.

"But it won't be easy, you know," Cal said. "You've got a lot to learn. Especially now that Angus has decided you need to be battle ready. It's going to be hard work."

I didn't argue. "I'm a fast learner."

A smile twitched at the corners of his mouth, but he hid it, maintaining a serious face. "By the way, Torren is up and moving now." He stopped my excited questions with a hand. "He's better. Still sore. Unsure of some of the details."

"Is he still bound to me?" I couldn't help but hope that somehow, the healing process had set him free.

Cal shook his head sadly. "Yes. Based on what I can sense, I'd guess it's even stronger than before."

I deflated, my wish that Tor could separate from me and return to his own life disappointed. "We have to find a way to stop this. He needs to be free of me."

Cal held my hand and Moose pressed against me again, both lending me their strength. "We'll find something, Laney. We'll keep looking." I heard the promise in Cal's words and prayed he was right.

ACKNOWLEDGEMENTS

To my husband, thank you for everything you do to keep this world spinning when I'm lost in another, getting the stories out. To my boys, thank you for always making me laugh and your unshakeable belief in me. To my parents, my sister and my brother, thank you for putting up with me all these years and cheering me on. To my friends, thank you for the time you spent reading the early drafts, talking me through changes and filling in the plot holes. Finally, to every person in the Acorn Publishing Family, thank you for being a part of this dream come true.

ABOUT THE AUTHOR

K.A. Fox is a proud military brat who has lived all over the world but now calls the Midwest home. She uses her psychological training to facilitate successful negotiations at work and to convince her husband and three sons that she's always right. When not writing, she can usually be found hiding somewhere with a book and a bit of chocolate or chasing after her own adorable Hell Hound. Connect with her at www.imkafox.com and on Facebook at www.facebook.com/imkafox.

www.ingramcontent.com/pod-product-compliance
Lightning Source LLC
Chambersburg PA
CBHW032107180726
48284CB00002B/487